麥禾陽光 Sun&Wheat

一個溫暖、高質感、充滿趣味的閱讀環境，
帶給讀者一個全然不同的學習感受。

麥禾陽光 *Sun&Wheat*

一個溫暖、高質感、充滿趣味的閱讀環境，
帶給讀者一個全然不同的學習感受。

麥禾陽光 Sun&Wheat

一個溫暖、高質感、充滿趣味的閱讀環境，
帶給讀者一個全然不同的學習感受。

麥禾陽光 Sun&Wheat

一個溫暖、高質感、充滿趣味的閱讀環境，
帶給讀者一個全然不同的學習感受。

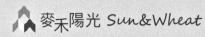

麥禾陽光 *Sun&Wheat*

一個溫暖、高質感、充滿趣味的閱讀環境,
帶給讀者一個全然不同的學習感受。

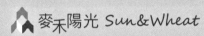

麥禾陽光 Sun&Wheat

一個溫暖、高質感、充滿趣味的閱讀環境,
帶給讀者一個全然不同的學習感受。

麥禾陽光

我是英語面試

人氣王 be NO.1

立馬擁抱理想工作！
掌握英語面試技巧，

A step-by-step GUIDE
to a WINNING INTERVIEW.

作者 徐 [維克]

 附MP3

英語面試成功 know-how 大公開
簡易三步驟、依樣畫葫蘆就對了！

履歷、自傳想破頭卻不知從何下筆；

面試QA該怎麼準備才能答得又快又好？

關鍵123，輕鬆寫出PRO級的履歷、自傳 & 自薦信。

掌握面試穿著禮儀，讓你的好感度瞬間激升不NG！

QA Time主題練習、靈活運用，口試不再 "皮皮挫"。

面試實錄大透析帶你更精確掌握各行各業的口試內容。

瞭解**國內外百大企業**，增加你談話的深度與廣度！

我就是跟別人不一樣，因為我是**英語面試人氣王**！！

推薦序

　　求職這條路想要走得順利，有許多的技巧一定要知道，想辦法讓自己比別人多出一些的優勢，自然能夠把其他的競爭者給比下去。在台灣目前的就業市場中，學歷不再是唯一的加分關鍵，擁有**相關證照**與**優秀的語言能力**，絕對能幫自己大大的加分，尤其是對那些想要進入大企業的求職者來說更是如此。談到語言，目前職場上最基本的就是英語，如果在面試這關就能表現出你在這方面的優勢，能從容地、有條理地用英文對答，那你一定能得到主考官的青睞。

　　《我是英語面試人氣王 A Step-by-step GUIDE to a WINNING INTERVIEW》將求職步驟簡化，不管是準備履歷表或是自傳都只要跟著步驟123，就能輕鬆完成。還有令許多求職者頭痛的英文面試以Q&A的方式呈現，再以各種主題做出區分，讓求職者方便搜尋所需資訊，Q&A的內容附有MP3，求職者能自主練習，讓應答更流暢，書末還附上一些百大企業的資訊，提供求職者參考。

　　我想大家在看完這本書後絕對會有大大的收穫，雖說現在大環境不景氣，但只要讓自己充滿競爭力，相信各位一定也能找到心之嚮往的工作，並在該職場中好好發揮所長，讓自己發光發熱。

104 人力銀行董事長

楊基寬

目錄

Chapter 1　面試前我該做哪些準備?

Chapter 2　面試技巧 Q&A Time

Chapter 4　百大企業故事看板

使用說明

將找工作分成4個部份,從書面資料準備開始,接著進行面試QA問答,再來要了解一些國內百大企業的故事,讓自己對企業的了解更深入!

在篇名頁的部份,可以看到接下來會討論到的主題有哪些。

Chapter 1 是說明如何準備書面資料,有3個步驟,順著箭頭指示就能照著寫出來囉!

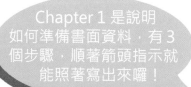

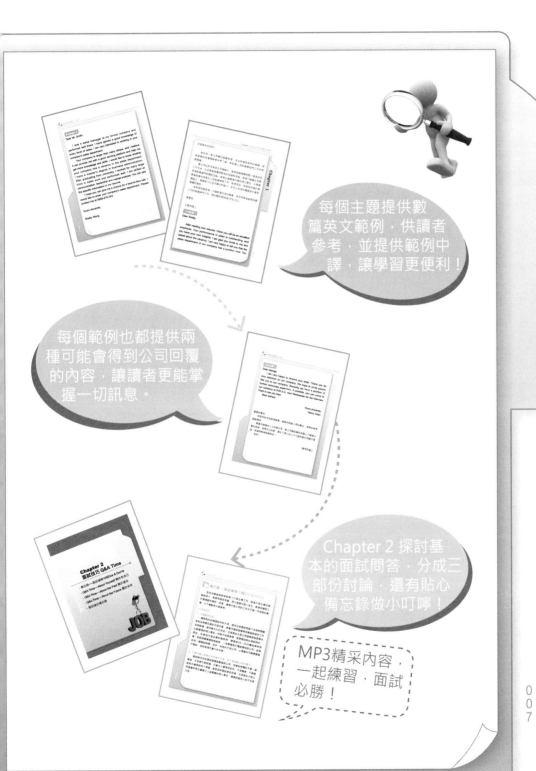

每個主題提供數篇英文範例，供讀者參考，並提供範例中譯，讓學習更便利！

每個範例也都提供兩種可能會得到公司回覆的內容，讓讀者更能掌握一切訊息。

Chapter 2 探討基本的面試問答，分成三部份討論，還有貼心備忘錄做小叮嚀！

MP3精采內容，一起練習，面試必勝！

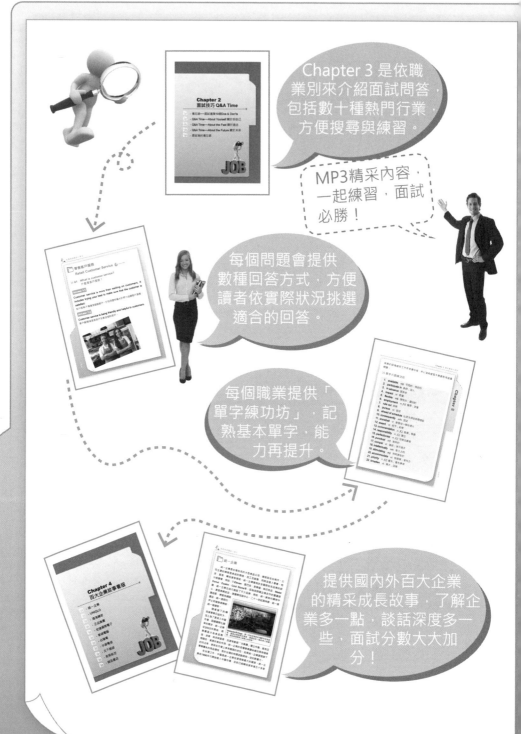

Chapter 3 是依職業別來介紹面試問答，包括數十種熱門行業，方便搜尋與練習。

MP3精采內容，一起練習，面試必勝！

每個問題會提供數種回答方式，方便讀者依實際狀況挑選適合的回答。

每個職業提供「單字練功坊」，記熟基本單字，能力再提升。

提供國內外百大企業的精采成長故事，了解企業多一點，談話深度多一些，面試分數大大加分！

Chapter 1
面試前我該做哪些準備？

JOB

📁 詢問職缺信

》 Step 1 How to Write

1. 首先說明信函目的，表明自己對該公司的興趣。
2. 文章主體主要介紹自己的技能、成就、經驗等，使用的文字應簡練、態度要表現積極。也可以就該公司的某方面進行闡述，表達自己的見解，引起對方的興趣。
3. 最後懇求對方能夠給予面對面討論以及面試職位的機會，表達感謝和期望。
4. 附上自己的聯繫方式。

》 Step 2 Practical Sentences

1. I am very interested in your company, and your corporate culture attracts me a lot. Therefore, I have searched for some information about your company.
   我對貴公司非常感興趣，貴公司的企業文化非常吸引我，因此我找了些資訊，以便更了解貴公司。

2. I have a master's degree in business administration. After graduating from university, I worked in sales for many large firms, and achieved good performance reviews.
   我有企業管理方面的碩士學位，大學畢業以後，我替許多大型公司從事銷售業務工作，並且有優秀的業績。

3. I hope you can give me a chance for a face-to-face talk.
   我希望您能給我一次面對面會談的機會。

4. Thank you in advance for your help.
   先謝謝您的幫助。

5. I think I am very suitable for your company. I hope you can provide me with an opportunity for employment.

我覺得自己非常適合貴公司。希望您能提供我就業的機會。

6. I am looking forward to working with you to discuss design issues as well as my career planning. I hope you will give me the chance to have an interview.

我期待能與您討論關於設計方面的議題，以及對自己職業生涯的規劃。希望您能給我一次面試的機會。

7. I am skilled in communication and am good at leading and market analysis. You can see the specific information on my resume.

我具有很強的溝通能力、領導能力以及市場分析能力。具體的資訊可以在我的履歷表中看到。

8. I know much in this area, and I have also participated in many small and medium-sized corporate forums, a variety of related competitions, and have achieved many awards.

我對這方面有很多的了解，也參加了很多中小企業論壇和各種有關的比賽，且獲得很多獎項。

9. I also worked as a manager of the customer service department in other companies, so I have some ideas to share with you.

我在別的公司也擔任過客服部經理的職位，所以我有些想法希望跟您分享。

10. I am looking forward to your reply. I hope I can get a job interview. If it is convenient for you, please contact me. My phone number is 2323-5172.

我非常期待您的回覆。我希望可以獲得一個面試的機會。如果您方便的話，請與我聯繫。我的電話是2323-5172。

》 Step 3 Examples

Example 1

Dear Mr. Chen,

I am a graduate student at National Taiwan University. I am majoring in corporate management. I am very interested in your company, and your corporate culture attracts me a lot. Therefore, I have searched for information about your company. I am going to graduate from school soon. I would like to ask if your company has any vacancies. I really hope to work for your company.

While I was at university, my research was mainly about the operation and management of small and medium-sized companies. I have participated in many small and medium-sized corporate forums and have competed in a variety of related competitions. I have received many awards.

I had a short-term summer internship in your company. During internship, I accumulated a lot of experience and knowledge. I think I am very suitable for your company. I hope you can provide me with an opportunity for employment.

I am looking forward to your reply and I hope to get a job

interview. If it is convenient for you, please contact me. My phone number is 2829-4521.

Yours sincerely,

George Huang

陳先生您好：

　　我是臺灣大學的研究生，主修是企業管理。我對貴公司非常感興趣，貴公司的企業文化非常吸引我，因此我蒐集一些關於貴公司的資料。我即將畢業，想詢問貴公司是否有職位空缺。我非常希望到貴公司工作。

　　我在大學期間主要研究的是中小企業的經營與管理。我參加了很多中小企業論壇和各種相關的比賽。我獲得了很多獎項。

　　暑假的時候也曾在貴公司短期地實習過。在實習期間，我累積了很多知識和經驗。我覺得自己非常適合在貴公司發展。希望您能夠提供我一個就業的機會。

　　我非常期待您的回信，而且我希望可以獲得一個面試的機會。如果可以的話，請聯繫我。我的電話是2829-4521。

真摯地，

黃喬治謹上

公司回覆 1

Dear George,

　　I am very happy to have received your letter. Thank you for the attention you have paid to our company. We hope to invite people like you to our company. We currently have a position open as human resources supervisor. Please come to our office at 9 a.m. next Wednesday for an interview. I hope to see you then.

Best wishes,

Henry Chen

親愛的喬治：

　　收到你的來信我很高興。謝謝你對敝公司的關注。我們非常希望能夠招聘像你這樣的人才來敝公司。敝公司最近剛好有個人力資源主管的空缺。請在下周三的上午九點來敝公司進行面試。希望到時候能看到你。

祝好，

陳亨利謹上

公司回覆 2

Dear George,

I have received your letter. Thank you for your compliments. It makes me feel very proud. I hope you can come for an interview, but we do not currently plan to hire new staff. I will keep an eye on this. Once there is a new vacancy, I will inform you immediately. I hope you can continue your work.

Best wishes,

Henry Chen

親愛的喬治：

你的來信我已經收到。謝謝你的讚美。這讓我感到非常驕傲。我非常希望你能來面試，但是目前我們沒有招聘新職員的計畫。我會幫你留意，一旦有新的職缺我會立即通知你。希望你繼續努力。

祝好，

陳亨利謹上

Chapter 1

Example 2

Dear Mr. Smith,

I was a sales manager at my former company and performed well there. I have gained a good knowledge of every facet of sales. I am very interested in working in your company's sales department.

Your company is larger than many others, and I believe it can provide me with a good working platform and help me get more knowledge and skills. I would like to know whether your company has a vacancy in the sales department. I have a master's degree in business administration. After graduating from university, I worked for many large firms in sales work and performed well. I am skilled at communication, leadership and market analysis. You can see the specific information in my resume.

I hope you can give me a chance for a face-to-face talk. I would like to enter your company's sales department. Please contact me at 0958-876-552.

Yours sincerely,

Shelly Wang

史密斯先生您好：

　　我在前一家公司擔任銷售經理，並在那裡有很好的業績。我對銷售的各個環節都非常了解。我對貴公司的銷售部門工作非常感興趣。

　　貴公司比許多其他公司規模大，我相信能夠提供我一個良好的工作平台，以及幫助我獲得更多的知識和技能。我想了解貴公司是否有銷售部門的職位空缺。我有企業管理方面的碩士學位。大學畢業後我曾在多家大公司做過業務工作，表現很好。我具有很強的溝通能力、領導能力以及市場分析能力。您可以在我的履歷表中看到具體的資訊。

　　我希望您能給我一次面對面交流的機會。我非常希望能夠到貴公司的銷售部門工作。我的電話是0958-876-552。

真摯地，

王雪莉謹上

公司回覆 1

Dear Shelly,

　　After reading your resume, I think you will be an excellent employee. Your performance in sales is outstanding, and you have your own insights. I am glad you wrote to me and asked about the vacancy. I am very happy to tell you that the sales department of our company has a position now. You can come for an interview the day after tomorrow if you like. The specific information has been posted on our company's website.

    I hope to see you.

Yours sincerely,

David Smith

親愛的雪莉：

    看過妳的履歷表後，我認為妳將會是一名非常優秀的員工。在銷售方面妳的表現非常突出，而且有自己獨特的見解。我很高興妳能寫信給我詢問職缺。我很高興地告訴妳，敝公司的銷售部門剛好有個職缺。要是妳願意的話，妳可以在後天來參加面試。具體的資訊已公布在敝公司的官網上。

    我希望到時候能見到妳。

真摯地，

大衛史密斯謹上

公司回覆 2

Dear Shelly,

    I am glad to tell you that we currently have a vacancy

in sales. However, this position is not very good. I am afraid it cannot meet your requirements; I don't know whether you would like to attend our interview. Our interview will start at 10 a.m. tomorrow. If you want to come, we will give you a warm welcome.

Yours sincerely,

David Smith

親愛的雪莉：

　　我很高興地告訴妳，敝公司目前有個銷售部門的職位空缺。但是，這個職位不是很理想。我恐怕這不符合妳的要求，不知道妳是否願意來參加我們的面試。我們的面試時間是明天早上十點。如果妳想來的話，我們非常歡迎。

真摯地，

大衛史密斯謹上

Example 3

Dear Ms. Jones,

　　I have been working as a designer for four years, and

I have worked for a lot of companies as a senior designer. I know your company is one of Taiwan's best design companies, so I would like to know if your company needs a designer.

I know this job needs strong professional knowledge. I have a master's degree in graphic design, and some of my works have won awards. What's more, I have a strong sense of responsibility, executive ability, and good team spirit. I am able to work well under high pressure.

I am looking forward to discussing design issues with you, as well as my career planning. I hope you can give me the chance to have a face-to-face interview. My telephone number is 2659-3125. Thank you in advance for your help.

Yours sincerely,

Marvin Lin

瓊斯女士您好：

　　我從事設計師工作已經四年，曾經在很多公司擔任資深設計師一職。我知道貴公司是臺灣是最好的設計公司之一，所以我想要了解貴公司是否需要一位設計師。

　　我知道這個工作要有很強的專業知識，我有平面設計的碩士學位，我的一些作品也獲得過獎項。同時我有很強的責任感、執行力

以及很好的團隊精神。我能夠在高度壓力下工作得很棒。

我期待能與您討論關於設計方面的議題，以及自己的職涯規劃。希望您能給我一個面對面的機會。我的聯繫電話是2659-3125。先感謝您的幫助。

真摯地，

林馬文謹上

公司回覆 1

Dear Marvin,

Many departments of our company are now hiring employees, including the human resources department, marketing department, financial department and the design department. There are many positions you can choose. But first of all, please send your resume and application letter to me. Then we will inform you of the specific time and place of the interview. Based on your good design foundation and experience, I think you can apply for the design department.

Yours sincerely,

Erica Jones

親愛的馬文：

　　敝公司現在有很多部門在招聘人員，包括人力資源部、營銷部、財務部及設計部。裡面有很多職位可以供你選擇。但首先，請把你的履歷表和求職信寄給我。然後我們會通知你具體的面試時間和地點。基於你有良好的設計基礎和經驗，我認為你可以應徵設計部。

真摯地，

艾莉卡瓊斯謹上

公司回覆 2

Dear Marvin,

　　Many departments of our company will soon hire new staff. Unfortunately, our design department doesn't have a plan to recruit new employees. If you would like to apply for a job in our company, I suggest that you have interviews in other departments, and then when the design department has any vacancies, you can transfer to design work. If you have other better choices, then I wish you good luck.

Yours sincerely,

Erica Jones

親愛的馬文：

　　敝公司的很多部門不久將招聘新人。很抱歉，我們的設計部沒有計畫招募新員工。如果你願意在敝公司應徵工作的話，我建議你先去別的部門面試，到時候設計部有空缺再調到設計部工作。如果你還有其他更好的選擇，那麼祝你好運。

真摯地，

艾莉卡瓊斯謹上

Example 4

Dear Mr. Chang,

　　I would like to know whether your company has a vacancy in the customer service department. I really want to join in this department of your company and to make a contribution to the company.

　　In order to know more about the department, I spent a few days doing a survey. I found that in the process of handling customers' inquiries and complaints, the staff was lacking in service skills, and their use of words was also short in flexibility. This often made the customer feel angry and will have a bad impact on your company's reputation.

　　I have worked as a manager of the customer service

department in other companies, so I have some ideas to share with you. I think the personnel of the department who deal directly with customers should be well trained and have a good service concept. There should be a standard operating procedure in handling complaints, and we should make the customers feel that they are respected and understood. I think I have good work experience in this field, so I hope I can join your company and make some contributions.

If there should be a vacancy, please let me know. I really hope to have the opportunity for an interview. My number is 2734-5551. Thank you very much.

Yours sincerely,

Fiona Hsu

張先生您好：

我想了解貴公司是否有客服部的職位空缺，我非常想要加入貴公司的這個部門，為貴公司做些貢獻。

為了更加了解這個部門的情況，我用了幾天時間進行調查。我發現貴公司職員在應對客户詢問和客戶投訴的過程中缺乏服務技巧，而且他們的用字也缺少靈活性。這常會讓顧客感到生氣。且對於貴公司的聲譽有不好的影響。

我曾在別的公司擔任過客服部經理，所以我有些想法跟您分

享。我認為客服部的一線人員要進行良好的培訓，並擁有優質的服務理念。處理投訴過程應該要有一套標準流程，我們應該讓顧客感受到他們被尊重和理解。我覺得我在這方面有很好的經驗，所以我希望能夠加入貴公司，並做出一些貢獻。

如果有職位的空缺，煩請通知我。我真的希望有面試的機會。我的電話號碼是2734-5551。非常感謝。

真摯地，

許費歐娜謹上

公司回覆 1

Dear Fiona,

I'm glad you can provide us with your advice. I like people who are good at observation, just like you. Our company will have a small job fair next month, which includes the position you want to apply for. I hope I can meet you there. I will tell you the specific information next month. Good luck.

Yours sincerely,

Justin Chang

親愛的費歐娜：

　　我很高興妳能夠為敝公司提供意見。我非常喜歡像妳這樣善於觀察的人。我們公司在下個月有個小型的招募會，裡面包括妳想要應徵的職位。希望到時候能夠見到妳。具體的資料我會在下個月通知妳。祝好運。

真摯地，

張賈斯丁謹上

公司回覆 2

Dear Fiona,

　　Your opinions are very important to us. We appreciate your suggestions. Unfortunately, our company has no recruitment plan, but I will keep an eye on this. I think you will be a very good employee. If there is some new information, I will inform you immediately. Looking forward to your arrival.

Yours sincerely,

Justin Chang

親愛的費歐娜：

　　妳的意見對我們來說非常的重要，我們很感謝妳的建議。但是敝公司最近沒有招聘人員的計畫，不過我會幫妳留意。我覺得妳是個非常好的人才。如果有新的訊息，我會馬上通知妳。非常期待妳的到來。

真摯地，

張賈斯丁謹上

Chapter 1

NOTES

date:　　/　/

求職自薦信

▶▶ Step 1 How to Write

　　求職自薦信是向公司展示自己的第一步，好的求職信能夠給對方留下深刻印象，進而為求職者贏得面試機會，因此寫好求職信非常重要。

　　求職自薦信的內容應該注意以下事項：

1. 求職信要寫明個人的地址、寫信日期和收信人的姓名、地址。

2. 文章中的稱呼要正式，最好要具體，這樣可以拉近與收信人之間的距離；如果不知道收信人是誰，則一般要用「先生 / 女士」。

3. (1) 第一段要表明自己寫信的目的、應徵的職位及職位訊息來源，態度要誠懇友善。

   (2) 第二段說明自己的能力和優勢，特別要針對自己所申請的職位要求，畢業生可以強調自己的學習成績、在校擔任過的幹部和實習經驗，有工作經驗者還要強調工作經驗。

   (3) 第三段表現自己的強烈意願和希望，懇請招聘方給予面試機會，並讓對方相信自己的決心。

4. 文章最後切記要寫上自己的聯繫方式，便於招聘方聯繫。最後表達美好的祝願。

5. 一般的求職信都會附加履歷表，來幫助招聘者更好地了解應聘者的素質和能力。因此，附履歷表的話要註明。

▶▶ Step 2 Practical Sentences

1. I am writing to apply for the job that you posted in the newspaper.

我想要應徵您在報紙上刊登的工作。

2. I am very pleased to introduce myself to you and wish to apply for the job.
我很高興自我介紹，我希望能夠申請這份工作。

3. I am told that your company needs an executive secretary, and I am happy to introduce myself to you.
我得知貴公司要招聘一名行政秘書，很高興能在這裡介紹自己。

4. I have a good education background, which provides me with good knowledge about the job.
我有良好的教育背景，讓我對這份工作有很好的認識與了解。

5. I believe that my good education and rich work experience will help me do well in this job.
我相信我良好的教育和豐富的工作經驗能使我勝任這份工作。

6. I know the job asks for —— the abilities of problem-solving, leadership and communication. And I think I have all of these abilities.
我知道這份工作要求有解決問題、領導和溝通能力。我認為我具備這些能力。

7. I am a person with an outgoing personality, and I like to communicate with all the people around me.
我的性格開朗，而且我喜歡與周圍的人交流。

8. If given the chance, I promise that I will try my best to do the job and make contributions to the company.
如能被錄用，我保證會盡我所能做好這份工作，為公司做出貢獻。

9. Through my previous jobs, I gained a lot of practical experience about <u>marketing</u>.

   經由我之前的工作，我獲得了很多關於<u>市場行銷</u>的實際經驗。

10. My dream is to become <u>the best salesman in this field,</u> and I think your company can make my dream come true.

    我的夢想是成為<u>這個行業最優秀的銷售業務</u>，我認為貴公司可以幫助我實現這個夢想。

11. I will appreciate it if offered the opportunity to interview and discuss the information in detail.

    如果您能給我面試機會，討論細節問題，我將不勝感激。

12. Thank you for taking me into consideration for this vacancy.

    謝謝您考慮錄用我。

》》 Step 3 Examples

Example 1

Dear Sir or Madam,

　　I saw your advertisement for the position of sales manager in the newspaper. I think that I am competent in this position. According to the advertisement, the position requires a sales manager with abundant work experience. Moreover, the sales manager should know the demands of the market and have a personality which will get on well with other staff. Having worked as a sales manager for the last three years, I have confidence that I can do well in personnel management. Furthermore, I can put myself in others' viewpoints and grasp the trends of the market.

I would appreciate your time in reading my information, and if there is any additional information you require, please let me know. I would be grateful if you give me a reply. Enclosed please find my resume.

Regards,

Shirley Wu

先生 / 女士您好：

我在報紙上看到貴公司正在招聘銷售部經理。我覺得我可以勝任這份工作。職位要求銷售部經理需有豐富的工作經驗。此外，銷售部經理應該充分熟悉市場需求，而且團隊意識強。在過去三年擔任銷售部經理，我有信心我能做好人事的管理工作。還有我能設身處地地替別人著想，且善於捕捉市場動態。

非常感謝您看我的求職信，如果您還需要其他的資料請告訴我。如能得到您的回覆，我將不勝感激。隨信附上我的履歷表。

問候，

吳雪莉

公司回覆 1

Dear Shirley,

Thank you for your application. I believe you are a hard-working person. We have studied your resume and considered you a qualified applicant. Will you be able to come to our office at 10 a.m. on July 7? We hope to get your reply as soon as possible.

Regards,

Stephen Peters

雪莉妳好：

謝謝妳的申請。我相信妳是個努力工作的人。我們看過妳的履歷表，覺得妳是一位合適的人選。妳能在7月7日上午10點來我們公司一趟嗎？我們希望能儘快得到妳的回覆。

問候，

史蒂芬彼得斯

公司回覆 2

Dear Shirley,

Thank you for your application. With comprehensive consideration, we are very sorry to tell you that you are not fit for this position. There is no doubt that you have excellent work experience, but this position requires a lot of travel on business, so we prefer a person who is able to. Please understand this.

Regards,

Stephen Peters

雪莉妳好：

謝謝妳的申請。經過慎重的考慮，非常遺憾妳不太適合我們的職位需求。妳的工作經驗豐富，這無庸置疑，但是這個職位需要經常出差，所以我們需要能配合出差的人。請理解這件事。

問候，

史蒂芬彼得斯

Example 2

Dear Sir or Madam,

I have learned from the job market of your vacancy for an administrative assistant. I'm quite interested and would like to apply for the post.

I will graduate from Fu Jen Catholic University in June of this year, majoring in Chinese. During the last four years, I've been studying hard and earnestly. I have both a computer skills certificate and an English certificate, making me proficient in computer software and English. In addition, as the chairperson of the Students' Organization, I have an open personality and am good at getting along with people around me. The most important thing is that I have excellent organizational and coordination abilities. I'm confident that I am fully prepared for this job. I'm looking forward to your reply. Enclosed please find my resume.

Sincerely,

Vanessa Lin

先生 / 女士您好：

我在就業市場了解到貴公司在招聘行政助理。我非常感興趣，

想應徵此職位。

　　我今年6月將從輔仁大學中文系畢業。在校四年，我學習認真刻苦。我有電腦技能證照和英文證照，能夠熟練操作電腦軟體並具有出色的英語聽說能力。另外，我是學生會主席，性格開朗，善於與周圍的人相處。最重要的是我具有出色的組織和協調能力。我非常有自信我已為這份工作做好充分準備。期待您的回信。隨信附上我的履歷表。

誠摯地，

林凡妮莎

公司回覆 1

Dear Vanessa,

　　We have received your resume. Your professional skills and the work experience in the Students' Organization are exactly what we expect. We sincerely invite you to come to our company to have an interview at 2 p.m. next Tuesday. Please bring your ID and the certificates with you. Please inform us if you can't come.

Yours sincerely,

Howard Cheng

凡妮莎妳好：

　　我們已經收到了妳的履歷表。妳的各項專業技能和學生會的工作經驗正是我們公司所期望的。我們誠摯地邀請妳於下周二下午兩點來公司進行面試。請妳攜帶妳的身分證和證照。如果妳不能來，請通知我們。

誠摯地，

鄭霍華德

公司回覆 2

Dear Vanessa,

　　Thank you for your application. You are an excellent student from a very famous university, but I am sorry to tell you that we prefer English majors for this position. However, we will keep your resume in our talent bank. We will contact you if we have positions that suit you in the future. Thank you again for your applying. I hope you have a bright future.

Yours sincerely,

Howard Cheng

凡妮莎妳好：

　　謝謝妳對敝公司的關注。妳是一位知名大學的優秀學生，但很遺憾，我們更傾向聘請英文系的學生。我們將會把妳的履歷表存放於我們的人才庫中。如果日後有合適的職位，會再與妳聯繫。再次感謝妳的應徵申請。祝妳前程似錦！

真摯地，

鄭霍華德

Example 3

Dear Sir or Madam,

　　Having heard of the recruitment of an accountant in your company, I wish to offer my services. I am currently a student at Sun Yat-sen University, majoring in accounting. I have been working hard and doing well in the academic main courses. I have a good understanding of accounting and tax regulations, and I am familiar with accounting procedures and regulations. I also have good computer skills and am skilled in communication. I have an open personality and a good understanding of team spirit. The rigorous and realistic style of your company attracts me deeply. I believe that your firm will be able to provide me with the right environment so that I can excel further.

I solicit the favor of an interview, and assure you that if appointed, I will do my best to satisfy you. Enclosed please find my resume.

Sincerely yours,

Carol Chuang

先生 / 女士您好：

　　據悉貴公司欲招聘會計師，我真心希望能貢獻我的服務。目前我是中山大學的在校生，主修會計學。我非常努力學習主修課並取得優異成績。我精通會計學、稅收條例，並熟悉會計程序與法規。我也熟練掌握電腦的操作，也很擅長溝通。我性格外向、團體意識強。貴公司嚴謹求實的作風深深地吸引了我。我相信貴公司能提供我良好的環境，這樣我就能有所突破。

　　我真心地希望您能給我一次面試的機會，若能有幸成為貴公司的一員，我一定不會讓您失望。隨信附上我的履歷表。

真摯地，

莊卡洛

Chapter 1

公司回覆 1

Dear Carol,

Thank you for your attention to our company. We were deeply impressed by your resume. We would like to invite you to an interview on May 5th at 3 p.m. Please be on time and inform us if you can't make it.

Regards,

HR Department

卡洛妳好：

感謝妳對本公司的關注。你的履歷表給我們留下了深刻的印象。特邀請妳於5月5日下午三點來參加面試。請準時參加，如不能參加，請通知我們。

問候，

人力資源部

公司回覆 2

Dear Carol,

Many thanks for your attention to our company. I'm sorry to tell you that you are not fit for our position. There is no doubt that you have an excellent education background, but our position requires at least two years' work experience. We don't have any positions for fresh graduates right now.

Best regards,

HR Department

卡洛妳好：

感謝妳對本公司的關注。我們非常抱歉，妳並不適合這個職位。毫無疑問妳有優秀的教育背景，但本職位需要有至少兩年的工作經驗。我們目前沒有針對應屆畢業生的職位。

真摯地，

人力資源部

Example 4

Dear Sir or Madam,

I have learned from the advertisement in the newspaper that your company is searching for a secretary. I am very interested in this position.

I am a graduate of Taiwan University, majoring in administrative management. My professional knowledge is very solid. I have strong communication and analysis abilities. I am also good at writing both in Chinese and English. As a class representative, I know the importance of coordination, and I believe I will do well in this job. I have broad interests in various fields, such as literature, music and history. I treat life with optimism, confidence and enthusiasm. I have the confidence that if given the chance, I won't make you regret your choice.

I am looking forward to getting an opportunity to have an interview. Please call me at 0910-002-234 if it is convenient for you. Thank you for your consideration. Enclosed please find my resume.

Sincerely,

Eason Chen

先生 / 女士您好：

　　我在報紙上看到貴公司招聘秘書的廣告。我對這份工作很感興趣。

　　我在臺灣大學主修行政管理。我的專業知識很紮實。我有很強的溝通和分析能力。我也擅長中英文作文。我曾任班代，知道協調工作的重要性，我相信我在這工作能做得很好。我的興趣廣泛，愛好文學、音樂和歷史。我的個性樂觀、自信，生活態度熱情。我相信如果能有這個機會，我一定不會讓您失望。

　　我很期待能夠獲得面試的機會。如果您方便的話，請聯繫我，我的電話號碼是0910-002-234。謝謝您的考慮！隨信附上我的履歷表。

真摯地，

陳伊森

公司回覆 1

Dear Eason,

　　Thank you for your applying for this position. After reading your resume, I would like to invite you to attend the interview on May 7th at 9:00 in the morning. Please bring a recent photo of yourself when you come. We are looking forward to meeting you.

Sincerely,

HR Dept.

＝＝＝＝＝＝＝＝＝＝＝＝＝＝＝＝＝＝＝＝＝＝＝＝＝＝＝＝＝＝＝

伊森你好：

　　非常感謝你應徵我們的職位。看過您的履歷表後，我們非常樂意邀請您在5月7日上午9點到敝公司進行面試。如能到訪，請攜帶一張你個人的近照。我們期待與你的會面。

誠摯地，

人力資源部

公司回覆 2

Dear Eason,

Thank you for your applying for this position. We think you would be a great fit for this position, but we are sorry to tell you that the vacancy has been filled. It is our pity not to have the opportunity to work with you. We will give priority to you if there is another chance in the future.

Regards,

HR Dept.

伊森你好：

　　非常感謝你應徵我們的職位。你是適合這一職位的難得人才，但是很遺憾告訴你，這個空缺最近已經補人。不能和你一起工作是我們的遺憾。以後如果還有工作機會，我們會優先考慮你。

問候，

人力資源部

Example 5

Dear Sir or Madam,

　　My adviser, Professor Lenard of Tsing Hua University, informed me that you are looking for a personnel manager, and I am extremely interested in this position.

　　I graduated from Tsing Hua University three years ago. Though I majored in administrative management, I am very interested in human resources management. I read a lot of books and studied human resources management on my own back in school. I have been working in the human resources department in other companies since I graduated, so I have gotten a lot of know-how about this field. If I get this job, I will try my best to satisfy you and make contributions to the company.

I am looking forward to an interview. Please contact me at 0911-145-303 if it is convenient to you. Thank you for your consideration. Enclosed please find my resume.

Sincerely,

Nicolas Tsai

先生 / 女士您好：

我的導師——清華大學的萊納德教授——告訴我，貴公司正在招聘一名人事主管，我對此很感興趣。

我三年前畢業於清華大學。儘管我主修行政管理，但是我對人力資源管理很感興趣。在學校時，我讀了很多書籍，也自學了很多這方面的知識。畢業後，我一直在其他公司的人力資源部門工作，因而在這方面我獲得很多訣竅。如果能夠得到這份工作，我一定盡最大努力讓您滿意，並為公司做出貢獻。

我期待能獲得面試的機會。如果方便的話，請聯繫我，我的電話號碼是0911-145-303。謝謝您的考慮。隨信附上我的履歷表。

真摯地，

蔡尼古拉斯

公司回覆 1

Dear Nicolas,

Thank you for paying attention to our company. We have studied your resume and decided that you are a qualified applicant. We want to have a face-to-face interview with you, so we can make our final decision. Will you be able to come to our company on Dec. 11th at 11:00 in the morning? Please let us know if you can't attend on time.

Regards,

HR Dept.

尼古拉斯你好：

　　謝謝你對敝公司的關注。看過你的履歷表後，我們覺得你是一位合適的人選。我們還需要和你進行一次面對面的會談才能做出最後的決定。12月11日上午11點你能來敝公司進行面試嗎？如果無法準時參加的話，請通知我們。

問候，

人力資源部

公司回覆 2

Dear Nicolas,

Thank you for paying attention to our company. After comprehensive consideration, we are sorry to tell you that you are not suitable for this position. You really have an excellent education background and rich work experience, but you job-hop too frequently. We need a person who can work with us for a long time. Please understand us.

Best regards,

HR Dept.

尼古拉斯您好:

謝謝你對敝公司的關注。經慎重考慮,我們很遺憾通知你並不符合這個職位的要求。你確實有不錯的學業背景和工作經驗,但是你跳槽過於頻繁。我們需要一個能長期與我們一起工作的人。請理解我們的決定。

此致敬意,

人力資源部

英文自傳

>> Step 1 How to Write

　　歐美的求職市場雖然並不要求自傳，但是臺灣的求職市場仍然相當重視自傳的內容。自傳是面試官了解求職者是否合乎企業需求的重要方式之一，決定能否獲得面試的機會。透過自傳可以了解求職者的思維模式、表達能力，以及更深入了解求職者的所學所能。

1. 可以強調相關學歷，可將自己在校所學，與應徵的職務緊密相扣，敘述修過的課程或好成績。如果工作與本科系所學無直接關連，則可陳述相關證照或曾經選修、旁聽的相關課程。

2. 可藉由過去的工作、社團經驗來呈現個人特質。如果學生時期的兼職經驗和應徵的職位沒有直接關連，則可以用個性和態度上的共同性來加強，凸顯與該職務的關連。

3. 再次強調性格上的競爭力，可多表達個人的學習精神及企圖心，如勤奮、積極、樂於學習等特質，並懇請給予面試機會。

>> Step 2 Practical Sentences

1. I graduated from Taiwan University of Science and Technology, and I majored in business administration.
   我畢業於台科大，主修企業管理。

2. I am optimistic and active, and I am confident that I am very suitable for this job.
   我是個樂觀而且活潑的人，我有自信我非常適合這份工作。

3. I hope I can be granted an opportunity for an interview.
   我希望能夠得到一個面試的機會。

4. I consider myself a person who is <u>easy to get along with</u>.
   我自認是一個<u>很好相處的</u>人。

5. Along the way, I combined the theory, experiments, and everyday life together.
   一路上，我把理論、實驗和日常生活結合在一起。

6. I hope you will keep me in mind for a possible opening.
   我希望如果有空缺的話，您能記得我。

7. I appreciate you for taking the time to review my autobiography.
   感謝您花時間審視我的自傳。

8. I focused on <u>marine transportation</u>.
   我特別集中在<u>海運</u>上。

9. But the most important thing is that <u>I never stop seeking knowledge</u>.
   更重要的是，<u>我從不停止追求知識</u>。

10. I will do my best to <u>learn more about every part of the company</u>.
    我會盡力<u>學習公司每一項事務</u>。

⟫ Step 3 Examples

Example 1

After finishing the military service, I tried to find a challenging goal for myself. I decided to take the GEPT High-Intermediate Level exam. Just as I thought, I passed the test with flying colors.

Chapter 1

I graduated from Taiwan University of Science and Technology, and I majored in business administration. I devoted myself to my studies and paid attention to all the details in school and in life. In school, I learned a lot from Mr. Wang, my favorite professor. He is my good friend and often helps me with great suggestions.

Also, my father is a good consultant to me. He always say, "I didn't have a good education, but you will." He has given me a lot of support and encouragement. I was born in Pingtung County, and we have lived by fishing for many generations. There are four people in my family. My mother is a housewife, and my little brother is a college student.

I am optimistic and active, and I am confident that I am very suitable for this job. I appreciate you for taking your precious time to read my autobiography. I hope I can be granted an opportunity for an interview.

　　在完成兵役之後，我試著為自己找到一個挑戰的目標。我決定報考全民英檢的中高級。就如同我想的一樣，我高分通過了測試。

　　我畢業於台科大，主修企業管理。我全心在學業上，而且注意學校與生活中所有的細節。在學校，我從我最喜愛的王教授那裡學到很多。他到現在仍是我的好朋友，而且經常提供我寶貴的建議。

　　我的父親對我來說，同樣也是一位好導師。他總是說：「我沒受好的教育，但你會有。」他給了我非常多的支持與鼓勵。我出生在屏東縣，好幾代都是以補魚為生。家中有四個人，我的母親是家

庭主婦，而弟弟是大學生。

我是個樂觀而且活潑的人，我有自信我非常適合這份工作。感謝您用您寶貴的時間來閱讀我的自傳。我希望能夠得到一個面試的機會。

Example 2

I was born in Kaohsiung City and grew up there. I consider myself a person easy to get along with. There are five people in my family. Both my parents are retired. One of my elder brothers is in charge of the import and export business in a big company. The other is a journalist for a magazine.

I believe that I was quite fortunate during the time I studied in school. In university, I learned everything I should learn, which helped me a great deal while I was doing research in graduate school. My professor, Mr. Jones, taught me one thing: "No matter how complicated the work is, you can always find the key through the basics." During my two years in graduate school, I started from basic mechanics. Then, I got a research project from a technology company, and that became the topic of my thesis. Along the way, I combined theory, experiments, and everyday life together. I got to know that R&D work would be my future career.

I hope for a smooth and stable life. I am not the kind of person who strives for fame and wealth. However, I am very ambitious to be a good researcher. That is why I have chosen to apply for this job. I think this job and its work environment can provide me with what I want. I really hope I can be a part of your team.

我在高雄市出生，並在那裡長大。我自認是一個很好相處的人。我的家裡有五個人，我的雙親都已退休，我有一個哥哥在一間大公司負責進出口業務，而另一個哥哥則是雜誌的記者。

我相信我在學校的求學過程相當地幸運。在大學中，我學到了所以應該學習的知識，這對於我在研究所進行研究時助益很大。我的教授瓊斯先生，教了我一件事：「無論工作有多麼的複雜，你一定可以從基礎中找到關鍵。」在研究所的兩年裡，我從基礎力學開始。然後我得到大公司的一份研究專案，這成為了我的論文主題。一路上，我把理論、實驗和日常生活結合在一起。我了解到，研發工作就是我未來的職涯所在。

我希望一個平穩安定的生活。我並不是汲汲於名利的那種人。然而，我非常有企圖心要成為一名優秀的研究員，這就是為什麼我選擇申請這份工作。我認為這份工作以及工作環境可以提供我想要的。我真的希望能夠成為您團隊的一分子。

Example 3

Recently I graduated from college, and I am eager to find a job that will offer me opportunities and changes. I hope you will keep me in mind for a possible opening.

I am an optimistic, dynamic and honest person. I majored in the hospitality industry, and I grasped all the principles. I also worked very hard to improve my English ability. Not only have I passed the Advanced Level of GEPT, but most importantly I can communicate with people comfortably in English. My ability to write and speak English is excellent. Moreover, I had several part-time jobs, during which I learned a lot about the hospitality industry.

I appreciate you for taking your time to review my autobiography. If there is any additional information you need, please feel free to contact me. I would truly welcome an opportunity to meet with you for an interview.

我最近從大學畢業，而我非常希望找到一份工作，可以提供給我機會和改變。我希望如果有空缺的話，您能記得我。

我是一個樂觀、有活力並誠實的人。我主修餐旅服務業，而我掌握各種原則。我也很努力提升我的英文能力。我不只通過了全民英檢高級檢定，更重要的是，我能和人以英文輕鬆地溝通。我的英文寫作和口說能力是很棒的。另外，我有幾次打工的經驗，而我從中學到了很多餐旅服務業的東西。

感謝您花時間審視我的自傳。如果有任何其他您需要的資料，請放心與我聯繫。我非常樂意接受一個面試的機會與您面談。

Example 4

My name is Janie Lin. There are four people in my family. I am the second child. My father is a government employee, and my mother is a teacher. My brother works in a bank.

I have always been a good student. Entering the university was a high point in my life. I had already decided my future goals, and I majored in shipping and transportation management. I focused on marine transportation. I especially liked my classes in shipping management, charter parties and tramp shipping.

I am a responsible, positive, patient person. I have a lot of marine transportation knowledge and an excellent work attitude. I believe that I can do everything well, but the most important thing is that I never stop seeking knowledge.

If you give me an opportunity to work for your company, besides my responsibilities, I will do my best to learn more knowledge about everything in the company.

Sincerely,

Janie Lin

　　我的名字是林珍妮。我家裡有四個人，我排行老二。我的父親是公務員，我的母親是老師。我的哥哥則在銀行上班。

　　我一直都是好學生。進入大學對我而言是個重要的時機。我已經決定了我未來的目標，我主修航運管理，我特別集中在海運上。我特別喜歡航運管理、租船合同以及不定期航運的課程。

　　我是個負責、正面、有耐心的人。我有很多的海運知識以及良好的工作態度。我相信我可以做好每件事，但最重要的是，我從不停止追求知識。

　　如果您給我一個到貴公司工作的機會，除了我個人的工作責任之外，我會盡力學習公司所有事務的知識。

真摯地，

林珍妮

date:　　　/　/

英文履歷表

》英文履歷表的細節內容

現在許多單位都希望求職者有比較紮實的英文基礎，特別是外商企業和對外交往比較多的單位，一份漂亮的英文履歷表會幫助你給對方留下很好的印象。

英文履歷表因其專業性與規範性，使得很多人一說到製作英文履歷表就頭痛，結果不是不敢寫，就是因為沒自信寫，白白喪失了很多機會。很多求職者只是簡單地翻譯一下中文履歷表，甚至有人直接利用翻譯軟體，可想而知，這樣的英文怎麼能給別人留下好的印象呢，更不用說深刻的印象了。其實製作一份英文履歷表並不難，你只要在製作英文履歷表時注意以下的幾個細節，一份優秀的英文履歷表很快就能出爐了！

1. 關於基本資料

英文和中文履歷表的元素其實差不多，主要包括以下幾個部分：

(1) Personal Information:

主要有Name、Contact Information等。如果有些人暫時還沒有英文名的話，用中文拼音也無妨，但切忌臨時取一個很滑稽的英文名，如Murderer（兇手）之類的。因為考慮到一些外商企業的網站服務器一般在國外，為了讓e-mail的溝通更加暢通無阻，建議使用Hotmail、Yahoo、Gmail等電子信箱。

(2) Career Objective:

職業目標簡介，同時兼顧入門工作以及長遠目標。如果你申請的職位與你的相關經歷和教育背景有直接的關係，這一部分可以省略。對於應屆畢業生來說這一部分可有可無。

(3) Education:

包括大學教育以及參加過的培訓。如果成績優秀，可以列出成績。至於主要課程，如果是為了充實頁面，可以考慮列出一些與應徵職位相關的課程。

(4) Work Experience:

對於每項工作，包括暑期實習和兼職，你應該列出以下資訊：公司名稱、工作時間、職位名稱或頭銜。對於其中某些與應徵職位相關的工作經驗，可以描述工作細節。為了<u>力求簡潔</u>，一般不使用整句，時態用<u>過去式</u>。

(5) Activities:

企業相當看重畢業生的社團活動經驗，具體寫法和 (4) Work Experience相似。

(6) Honors & Awards:

這也是企業比較關注的內容。獎項最好列三項以上，同時需要列出時間、名稱和頒發的單位。

(7) Skills:

主要是語言能力、電腦能力和個人特長，長度一般不要超過四行。

此外，求職者的姓名、性別、出生年月等，與中文履歷表大體一致。但要注意，在英文履歷表中，求職者受教育的時間排列順序與中文履歷表中的時間排列順序正好相反，也就是說，是從求職者的<u>最高教育學歷</u>寫起。在時間排列順序上亦遵循<u>由後至前</u>這一規則，即從當前的工作崗位寫起，直至求職者的第一個工作崗位為止。

2. 求職目標（應徵職位）的寫與不寫

　　關於求職目標有的人主張寫，有的人主張不寫。通常美式履歷表的規範製作方法都是不寫的。例如，求職者在申請加入一家著名公司時明確寫上了應徵的部門，那麼萬一這個部門沒有錄用你，而你又好像非應徵這個部門不可，你就很可能失去了選擇其他部門的機會。如果不寫的話，企業會參照你的背景和一些測試的結果也許認為你更適合別的部門，這樣你就可能獲得新的機會。一般，招聘單位會在招聘啟事中提示是否標明求職目標，所以求職者也可根據招聘單位的要求來選擇寫或不寫。

3. 內容有條理

　　面試官可能每天要看的履歷表不止上百份，目光停留在一份履歷表上的時間頂多不超過10~20秒的時間。因此建議將履歷表內容以條例方式呈現，讓招聘的人事在短短的時間內就能馬上抓住這份履歷表的重點。

4. 把「技能」寫清楚

　　求職者要將之前所服務單位的名稱、自身的職位、技能寫清楚。把社會工作細節放在工作經歷中，這樣會填補工作經驗少的缺陷。例如，在擔任社團幹部或學生會會長時，舉辦過什麼活動、聯繫過什麼事、參與過什麼都可以一一羅列。如果是應屆的（大學）畢業生，雇主通常並不指望你在暑期工作期間會有什麼驚天動地的成就；但現在其實有愈來愈多的學生會懂得在學期間就開始為自己的未來規畫、努力，如果是這樣的狀況，通常都能讓雇主留下深刻的印象哦！

5. 搭配求職信

　　求職信兼顧著自我推薦的責任，是製作英文履歷表不可或缺的搭檔。有了求職信，你的履歷表將威力倍增。

6. 列舉所獲獎勵和發表的作品

　　將自己所獲獎項及所發表過的作品列舉一二，可以從另一方面證實自己的工作能力和取得的成績。在陳述的時候，記得將獎學金等資料以逐行的方式來介紹，每一項獎學金或是獎勵用一行來表示。另外，大多數外商企業對英文（或其他語言）及電腦能力都有一定的要求，個人的語言水準、程度可在此列出說明。

7. 寫自己熟悉、有把握的

　　履歷表中的任何訊息，都可能成為面試中的話題，一定要寫熟悉的、有把握的，關於那些一知半解的就算了，不要給自己找麻煩。要實事求是，千萬不要誇張，外商企業最不喜歡撒謊的員工，一旦讓企業覺得你在撒謊，你就喪失了進入這間公司的機會。

8. 拼寫正確，避免明顯的語法錯誤

　　對母語不是英文的人來說，拼寫檢查要格外仔細。現在的很多文字處理軟體都有拼寫檢查功能，如果你犯了這類很基本的錯誤，企業可能會覺得你對最基本的東西都缺乏責任感，那怎麼敢用你呢？當然，因為英語畢竟不是我們的母語，所以要杜絕所有的語法錯誤也不太可能，只要不是太離譜的，稍微有點小錯，面試官也是可以諒解的。

　　此外，在英文的應用上，要注意避免一些地方：

(1) 長句：

　　沒有人願意看太冗長的句子，而且切記YRIS(Your resume

is scanned, not read) 原則，雇主只是在掃描你的履歷表。

(2) 縮寫：

因為外行人往往很難看懂。不要想當然地認為這是眾所皆知的事情。

(3) I：

因為正規履歷表中的句子多以動詞開頭，是沒有「我」的。當然若在公司簡介中一定要用到一兩次，也不是完全不可以。

(4) "Reference available upon request"：

這個短語的意思是如需證明，可提供見證人。這在許多英式履歷表範文中經常出現，但是美式的履歷表則不要這樣寫。

9. 注意相似的單詞

相似單詞出錯有時拼寫檢查都查不出錯誤，所以要尤其小心。比如：有一位主修是經濟學的求職者，他本應寫 Major: Economics（主修：經濟學）但卻誤寫成了 Mayor: Economy，詞意大變，變成了主管經濟的市長。

10. 根據自身情況調整項目

有時候你可能不一定非要寫出professional qualities（技能以及專長）這個項目，或甚至以summary（經歷概要）來加以代替。這些都完全取決於你自己的選擇。

11. 讓別人代替你檢查

這是非常有效的一個方法，一是從拼寫、語法、句式等方面來看，有無錯誤；二是從構思的角度上來看有沒有更合適、更恰當的

表達。旁觀者清，換個角度來看，旁觀者經常能提出一些特別好的建議。

》 英文履歷表的形式

　　英文履歷表是進入外商企業或取得高薪的敲門磚，製作一份好的履歷表就等於跨出了求職成功的第一步，求職者只要掌握英文履歷表撰寫技巧，勇於嘗試，堅持不懈，就一定會實現自己的目標！下面為大家簡單介紹一下英文履歷表的常見形式。

　　英文履歷表並無固定不變的單一形式，求職者完全可以根據個人的具體情況來確定採用何種形式，靈活設計。

　　一般來說，根據個人經歷的不同側重點，可以選用以下三種形式。

1. basic resume——以學歷為主的履歷表

　　這種形式適合應屆畢業生，因為沒有工作經歷，所以把重點放在學業上，從最高學歷往下寫。

　　在basic resume中，一般包括下列元素：

(1) personal date（個人資料）：
　　name（姓名）、address（通訊地址）、postal code（郵遞區號）、phone number（電話號碼）、birth date（出生日期）、date of availability（可到職日期）。

(2) job/career objective（應徵職位）

(3) education（學歷）：
　　就讀學校及科系的名稱、學位、起迄時間和應徵職位相關的課程與成績、課外活動、獎勵等都應一一列出。

(4) special skill（特別技能）

(5) hobbies/interests（業餘愛好）：
　　如果在學歷項目的課外活動中已經註明，此項則不必重複。

Example

Vincent Wang

No.23, Lane 34,
Sec. 6, Zhongxiao E. Rd.
Nangang Dist., Taipei City
0910-222-321
vincent.wang@yahoo.com

EDUCATION

Taiwan University
Bachelor of Business Administration, Sept. 2006~June 2010
Major: Business Administration
Minor: Spanish
- Average Grade: 85
- Several Scholarships
- Augusta Scholar's Award
Jianguo High School
- Chairperson of Students' Organization
- In charge of Guitar Club and Dance Club
- Leader of Basketball Team

SKILLS

- Computer Skills: Windows, MS Office, Adobe Illustrator, Photoshop
- Languages: Proficient in English and Spanish

PERSONAL INTERESTS

Travel, Politics, Reading, Cycling and Financial Markets

王文森

台北市南港區忠孝東路六段34巷23號

0910-222-321

vincent.wang@yahoo.com

教育背景

臺灣大學

企管學士，2006年九月～2010年六月

主修：企業管理

副修：西班牙文

- 平均成績分數：85
- 曾獲得多份獎學金
- 曾榮獲奧古斯塔學者獎

建國中學

- 學生會會長
- 吉他社社長及熱舞社社長
- 籃球隊隊長

技能
- 電腦技能：Windows、Office系列、Adobe Illustrator、
  Photoshop
- 語言：英文和西班牙文流利

個人興趣
旅行、政治、閱讀、騎自行車、財務金融市場

2. chronological resume——以經歷為主的履歷表

　　這種形式的英文履歷表，適合有工作經驗的求職人員。一般都是把和應徵職位有關的經歷和業績按時間順序寫出來，把工作經歷放在學歷之前。經歷和學歷的時間順序均是由近至遠。

　　在chronological resume中，通常包括以下元素：

(1) personal date（個人資料）：
　　具體內容和以學歷為主的履歷表基本一致。

(2) job/career objective（應徵職位）

(3) work experience（工作經驗）：
　　務必寫明自己在每個工作單位的職位、職責和業績以及工作起迄時間。

(4) education（學歷）：
　　既然已工作多年，雇主重點考慮就不是你的學歷，而是工作經驗。所以這部分不必寫得太詳細，只需註明你就讀的校系名稱、始迄時間和學位即可。

(5) technical qualifications and special skills
　　（技術資格和特別技能）

(6) scientific research achievements（科研成果）

Example

George Tang

No.38, Lane 55, Jiuquan St.

Datong Dist., Taipei City

0922-345-025

george.tang@hotmail.com

EXPERIENCE

Strategy Consultant: Tommy Consulting Group, Taipei, Nov. 2010~present
- Implemented delivery strategy
- Managed more than 20 work groups to improve business strategies

Human Resources Manager: Davidson, Inc., Taipei, Jun. 2005~Oct. 2010
- Supervised independent carriers and employees to obtain quality delivery to 32,000 households
- Trained new area managers
- Interviewed and contracted distribution agents
- Oversaw distribution of various products to 450,000 households

Supervisor: Oliver International, Taipei, Sep. 2000~May 2005
- Oversaw distribution and packaging of more than 200,000 products

- Created new route structure for delivery of products using mapping software

District Operator: Bridge Company, Taipei, Aug. 1997~Aug. 2000

- Maintained home-delivery and single-copy accounts
- Promoted sales and established routes in new growth areas
- Recruited and trained 20 employees
- Conducted audits for 12 district offices

QUALIFICATIONS

- Experience includes diverse managerial skills in distribution, planning and organizing
- Restructured two alternate delivery companies to obtain quality distribution, requiring the recruitment of a competent staff
- Highly competent with Windows, MS Office, Adobe Illustrator

EDUCATION

Tsing Hua University
Bachelor of Business Administration
Major: Economics

唐喬治

台北市大同區酒泉街55巷38號

0922-345-025

george.tang@hotmail.com

工作經歷

策略顧問：湯米顧問諮詢集團，台北，2010年十一月迄今

- 執行快遞策略
- 管理二十多個工作團隊，提升商業策略

人資經理：大衛森公司，台北，2005年六月～2010年十月

- 監督獨立運輸業者及員工，獲得三萬兩千戶的高品質快遞成果
- 訓練新任的地區經理
- 面談配送代理商及簽約
- 監督各類產品配送，共四十五萬戶

主管：奧立佛國際，台北，2000年九月～2005年五月

- 監督超過二十萬件產品的配送及包裝
- 使用繪圖軟體創建產品遞送的新路線規劃

區域執行：布立奇公司，台北，1997年八月～2000年八月

- 維持家戶遞送及散戶
- 提高業績並建立新成長區域的路線
- 招募並訓練二十名員工
- 審計十二所區域辦事處

資格

- 在配送、計畫、組織上的各種管理技巧富有經驗
- 重組兩家遞送公司，以獲得高品質遞送，需聘請有能力的職員
- 高度熟悉Windows、Office系列以及Adobe Illustrator等軟體

教育背景

清華大學

企管學士

主修：經濟學

3. functional resume——以職能為主的履歷表

　　這種形式的英文履歷表，也是突出工作經歷，所以所含元素和以經歷為主的履歷表相同。兩者之間的根本差別在於：以經歷為主的履歷表是按時間順序來排列工作經歷，而以職能為主的履歷表則按工作職能或性質來概括工作經歷，並無時間上的連貫性，旨在強調某些特定的工作能力和適應程度。

Example

Monica Chen

No.4-1, Lane 20, Changji St.

Datong Dist., Taipei City

0958-401-122

monica.chen@gmail.com

HIGHLIGHTS OF QUALIFICATIONS

- More than four years developing strategies and proposals for new product developments
- Extensive experience conducting research, writing, and presenting
- Led various initiatives in corporate strategic planning

PROFESSIONAL ACCOMPLISHMENTS

- **Sales:** As a salesperson at Johnson's Inc, persuaded decision makers within the government and business sectors to use our marketing software

- **Research & Development:** Worked with others on a novel essay which identifies the antibodies' ability to treat different cancers.
- **Presentation Skills:** At Peters Institute, responsible for conducting regular corporate updates on sector performance; promoted to sector manager after second year
- **Product Development:** Developed long-standing relationships with clients that ultimately increased firm revenue by 10% over three years (Johnson's Inc.)
- **Public Relations:** Handled media relations, explaining the organization's positions on current issues (Learning Resource Center)

EMPLOYMENT HISTORY

- Sales Coordinator: Peters Institute, 2006-2013
- Research Specialist: Learning Resource Center, 2000-2006
- Salesperson: Johnson's, Inc, 1998-2000

EDUCATION

National Cheng Kung University

Master of Business Administration, 1994-1998

- Focused on organizational structures and finance

Chapter 1

陳莫妮卡

台北市大同區昌吉街20巷4-1號

0958-401-122

monica.chen@gmail.com

專業資格

- 超過四年的經驗，為新產品發展建立策略及提案
- 豐富的研究、寫作、簡報經驗
- 領導先機，計畫公司策略

專業成就

- **銷售**：強森公司業務員，成功說服政府機關和企業公司的決策人員使用行銷軟體
- **研發**：合作編寫全新論文，說明抗體治療各類癌症的能力
- **簡報能力**：在彼得斯機構，負責常態的部門表現企業公報，第二年升任為部門經理
- **產品發展**：發展客戶長期關係，最終在三年內提升公司獲利百分之十（強森公司）
- **公共關係**：處理媒體關係，說明組織對於時事的態度（學習資源中心）

任職經歷

- 銷售協調員：彼得斯公司，2006-2013
- 研究專員：學習資源中心，2000-2006
- 業務員：強森公司，1998-2000

教育背景

國立成功大學

企業管理學士1994-1998

- 主攻組織構造及財務

date:　　　/　/

📁 備忘錄──面試穿著和禮儀

　　求職者在出發面試之前，必須檢視自己的衣著打扮是否合宜，俗語說「佛要金裝，人要衣裝」。合宜的穿著與裝扮，代表了個人的自我風格以及概念，除了給主考官良好的第一印象，肯定求職者的品味和能力，同時也顯示求職者的慎重態度。最重要的是，良好的第一印象就是成功的一半。

　　以下提供一般面試時較合宜的穿著方式，但仍然需要依照各種產業加以適度調整。

》男性

1. 男性的頭髮要注意修整，過長的頭髮應立即修剪。
2. 如果有戴眼鏡的話，記得要搭配自己的臉型。
3. 西裝要講究剪裁，不標新立異，傳統深藍、深灰色為佳。 西裝褲一般最好搭配深色，熨燙平整。
4. 一般而言應穿著西裝，搭配的長袖襯衫最好以白色為主。
5. 領帶的長度需及腰帶處。領帶的種類繁多，在搭配襯衫和領帶時，要注意色彩的協調和線條方向的一致。
6. 皮鞋的顏色最好和皮帶統一色調，避免呈現過於複雜。皮鞋務必擦拭光亮，襪子應著深色。

》女性

1. 髮型以清爽整潔、適宜臉型為主，可以染髮，但切忌勿染過份誇張的顏色。
2. 最好以剪裁大方、具有質感的套裝為首要考量，領口勿過低、裙長大約為膝蓋以上10公分以內。切忌穿著低胸、透明、緊身、露骨的衣服。

3. 飾品方面,戒指、耳環、項鍊、腰帶可視需要做一、二項選擇搭配,但數量不宜過多,另外手指甲記得修剪整齊。

4. 以淡妝為宜,上完粉底後,採眼、眉、唇重點式的化粧即可。

5. 最好穿著包頭式的高跟鞋,鞋跟的高度可依個人舒適度選擇,但最好勿穿平底鞋。因為穿上跟鞋,會讓自己看起來更為優雅,也會比較有精神。

面試不但是找工作,更是和一個陌生人見面會談的場合,所以基本的禮儀是必要的,以下有幾點在面試時必須特別注意:

1. 絕對不可以遲到,要事先預估到該公司可能花費多少時間,最好能比預定時間早到,可先了解該公司的周圍環境,並抒解緊張的心情。

2. 態度過於輕挑是絕對不被接受的,因此在面談時,千萬不要嚼口香糖、蹺腿、或是亂開玩笑。

3. 站姿與坐姿都需要留意,坐下面試時千萬不要很輕鬆地就靠著椅背,要挺背坐正,維持良好的儀態。

4. 不要賊頭賊腦地到處走動,窺視他人的上班情形。

5. 萬一面試官提起政治、經濟、社會、書籍等問題時,愈深入的話就愈容易引發爭論,所以盡量籠統地回答。

6. 不要用艱澀難懂的術語,其效果有可能反而產生負面印象。

7. 如果親友中有顯赫之人,不需要刻意提出來炫耀,只怕會適得其反。

8. 不要過於主動地詢問薪資待遇,最好等到對方詢問。

9. 自信但不要自滿,注意說話時的態度不要趾高氣昂。

NOTES

date: / /

Chapter 2
面試技巧 Q&A Time

- 備忘錄──面試達陣10個Dos & Don'ts

- Q&A Time──About Yourself 關於你自己

- Q&A Time──About the Past 關於過去

- Q&A Time──About the Future 關於未來

- 面試後的備忘錄

備忘錄——面試達陣10個Dos & Don'ts

很多求職者都希望能進入大型企業工作，因為大型企業的規模都很大，制度和規定完善，用人制度也很人性化，薪資待遇和工作環境都非常好。但是，應徵大型公司的工作也不是一件容易的事情，以下幾點供大家參考。

》Don't!

1. 不要遲到失約

遲到和失約是面試中的大忌。這往往給面試官留下沒有時間觀念和沒有責任感的不良印象，更會令面試官覺得求職者對這份工作沒有熱情，使印象分大打折扣。尤其是在大型公司這樣對制度要求比較嚴格的用人單位。守時不但是美德，更是面試時必須做到的。因此，在參加大型企業的面試時，應提前10～15分鐘或準時到達。如因有要事遲到或缺席，一定要提前打電話通知該公司，並預約另一個面試時間。另外，匆匆忙忙到公司，心情還未平靜便要進行面試，自然表現也會大失水準。

2. 不要評論之前單位及同事的不是，更不要譴責以前的雇主

面試時切勿在面試官面前數落前公司、同事和老闆的不是。這樣做，不但得不到同情，只會令人覺得你記仇、不念舊情、不夠寬容和不懂得與別人相處，甚至招來面試官的反感。尤其是在大型公司這種非常注重員工人品素養的用人單位，隨便評論別人的不足是大忌。

3. 不要說謊和誇耀自己

　　面試時說謊，偽造「歷史」、編造故事或將不屬於自己的功勞「據為己有」，後果可大可小。即使現在能瞞天過海，也難保謊言將來不會有被識破的一天。因此，面試時應實話實說，雖可揚長避短，卻也不能以謊話代替事實，誠實坦誠才能給面試官留下良好印象。

4. 不要準備不足就去參加面試

　　無論學歷多高、資歷多深、工作經驗多豐富，當面試官發現求職者對申請的職位認識不多，甚至連最基本的問題也回答不好，會給面試官留下專業知識和素質嚴重欠缺的不好印象，面試官不但會覺得求職者準備不足，甚至會認為他們根本無志於在這方面發展，所以面試前應做好充分的準備工作。

5. 不要長篇大論、喋喋不休

　　雖說面試是推銷自己的最佳時機，不過，切勿滔滔不絕、喋喋不休，面試官最怕求職者長篇大論，話說個沒完卻找不到重點。其實回答問題，只需針對問題重點回答。相反，有些求職者十分害羞，不懂得把握機會表現自己，無論回答什麼問題，答案往往只有一兩句，甚至只回答「是、有、好、可以」等，讓人感覺你很不健談，沒有自己的主見和想法，或是不善於表達自己的意見都是不可取的。如果性格膽小害羞，則應多加練習，以做到談吐自如。

6. 不要用過多語氣詞或口頭禪

　　使用太多如「呢、啦、吧」等語氣詞或口頭禪會把面試官弄得心煩意亂，使面試官產生厭煩情緒。另外，語氣詞或口頭禪使用太多也會讓面試官誤以為求職者自信心和準備不足。

7. 不要過多談論前任工作

　　不管你的前任工作做得如何，都不要過多談論和糾纏。一般來說，你只要說明你做過類似的事，有此方面的工作經驗即可，不必說工作的具體成績。如果你做得很好，為什麼要離開？如果做得很差，那你個人的能力肯定有問題。總之不管怎麼樣說，都可能會招來面試官的反感；所以就盡量輕輕帶過就好。

8. 不要給面試官留下沒有職業目標的印象

　　面試時，千萬不要給面試官留下沒有明確職業目標的印象。雖然一些求職者的其他條件很符合、也不錯，但無職業目標就會缺少進取心、主動性和創造性，給企業帶來損失。面試官倒情願聘用一個各方面表現雖較遜色，但具有事業目標和工作熱情的求職者！

9. 穿著不宜

　　求職者在服裝儀容部分，打扮須符合所應試職務的特性，避免奇裝異服、濃妝豔抹。有些人非常有自信，認為穿著與個人的工作能力沒有絕對的關係，但是你對面試官而言是一個陌生人，他無從得知你的工作能力，所以外表是絕對重要的。

10. 說話態度

　　有些人的態度過於自信，在面試官的眼中反而變成傲慢不佳；或有些人自以為幽默的無厘頭問答，試圖緩和自己緊張的心情以及面試的緊繃感，這些都是大忌。記得放鬆心情，以平常心和積極的態度面對即可。

　　求職者想要增加錄取機會，回答必須從容不迫、簡明扼要、恰

當中肯，可以看看以下幾方面建議：

》Do!

1. 事先調查

　　事先了解該公司的規模、在全球的活動概況等要事，包括總公司、分公司等業績表現、經營規模，以及今後打算開展的業務等。如無法得到書面資料，也要設法從該公司或其他同行中獲得情報。這樣才會在面試中得心應手，讓面試官感覺求職者很看重這份工作。

2. 準備妥當

　　準備好所有證書等，譬如與專業能力相關的資格證書，或參加培訓的資料，最好和應徵職務有直接關聯，不但可證明自己在這一方面所做的努力，也能向面試官表示自己具有這方面潛能。

3. 蒐集情報

　　面試時自我介紹內容應強調應徵的動機以及想應徵的職位，因此要蒐集好相關職位的情報，自我介紹時才能胸有成竹、信心滿滿、表達順暢、切合主題。

4. 3P原則(1)-Positive

　　回答問題時應該遵循「3P原則」，即Positive（自信）、Personal（個性）、Pertinent（中肯）。談吐自信，就是要積極地進行自我肯定，讓面試官充分了解你的優點與潛能。

5. 3P原則(2)-Personal

突出個性和優勢，就是要把自己與眾不同的特點發揮出來，強調自己的專業與能力，讓面試官感覺你是這個職位的最佳人選。

6. 3P原則(3)-Pertinent

語氣中肯，就是要實事求是，不要言過其實，誇張說話，也不要涉及和自己無關的事情。

7. 換句話說

靈活的求職者往往會把「我」開頭的話，變成「你」。例如：

面試官： "Will you please say something about yourself?"

（請你談談自己的情況好嗎？）

求職者： "Do you want me to talk about my personal life or to say something about the job?"

（你想讓我談談我個人的生活呢，還是與這份工作有關的問題？）

這種談話的方式所產生的效果是不言而喻的。面試畢竟是面試官與求職者互相溝通的一種場合，求職者時常把面試官融入自己的談話當中來，自然而然就起到了互相溝通的作用。

8. 自我介紹

自我介紹應簡潔明瞭，給面試官留下思路清晰、反應靈敏、邏輯性強的印象。自我介紹時間不宜過長，話語不宜過多，最好控制在5分鐘之內。不要一談起自己就口若懸河、滔滔不絕，以免言多語失。另外，在自我介紹時應避免過多地使用 I（我），不要每個句子一開頭就冒出一個 I 字，給面試官留下自我標榜、以自我為中

心的不良印象。

9. 表現自己

　　回答問題時口齒要清晰，語調和語速適中，內容要有條理，重點要突出，避免重複。介紹工作經歷要採用倒敘的形式，從最近一份工作談起，著重強調有利於新工作的職務經歷。最好能說明曾擔任何種職務、實際成績、業績等，以及自己的工作對原來公司的影響。凡和此次應徵不相關的內容，則要儘量避免提及。

10. 面試的話題

　　面試時談論的話題要緊扣三方面來展現自己的優勢。

　　當你了解到招聘單位急需用人時，首先要把自己的**專長**完全展現出來，然後順理成章地得出結論：「我想，貴單位需要像我這樣的人才。」用這樣的句子，會讓面試官認為你是站在他們的立場上說話，所以也就會更容易接受你。

　　陳述自己的任職資格時，求職者可以這麼開頭：

　　"I'm qualified for the job because..."

　　（我能勝任這項工作，是因為......）

　　接著陳述**理由**。當面試官在審視你究竟能不能勝任此職時，參照的標準已不再是他心目中的標準，而是你列舉的理由，有理有據地征服面試官。

　　真實的**業績**。尤其是遇到外商公司面試喜歡用事實說話，為了證明你的能力，你可以把過去的經歷聯繫起來，說明你曾經為以前的公司解決過跟現在面試官所面臨的類似問題：

　　"I explored Shanghai market and sold 50,000 sets in one year."

　　（我開發了上海市場，一年銷售了5萬套。）

真心誠意。當你對某個問題發表完見解之後，可以附帶加上一句：

"I'd like to know your opinion."

（我很想聽聽您的意見。）

→這句話就會向面試官表明你對他的尊敬，很容易使他對你產生親切感、信任感。

當面試官在試探你的誠意時，你應該及時表態：

"So far as that is concerned, you must have understood my determination."

（談到這裡，您一定已經明白我的決心。）

問些與工作內容相關的問題，能表現你對這份工作的興趣和熱情，例如：

"What other responsibilities do you think this job will include?"

（您認為這項工作還包括什麼其他的責任呢？）

Q&A Time—About Yourself 關於你自己

>> **Q1　Tell me something about yourself.**
　　請你做一下自我介紹。　 track 001

　　這是面試的必考題目，一般出現在面試的一開始。基本要求是要做到自我介紹的內容與履歷表一致，但自我介紹絕不僅僅是簡單地對個人履歷表的重複。在表述方式上要儘量口語化。內容上，要切中要害，不要太多不相關的內容。條理要清晰，層次要分明。

Answer 1

I am a person with strong interpersonal skills and have the ability to get along well with people. I enjoy facing challenges and looking for creative solutions to problems.

我的人際交往能力很強，與人相處得很好。我勇於迎接挑戰，對於問題，樂於尋找富有創造力的解決方法。

Answer 2

Besides the details given in my resume, I believe in character values, vision and action. I am quick in learning from mistakes. I am confident that the various tests that you have conducted will corroborate my aptitude and attitude for the job.

除了我在履歷表中的資料外，我相信性格的價值、眼光和行動。我善於快速地從失敗中學習。我有自信，您所做的測驗能夠佐證我的天賦以及我對這份工作的態度。

Answer 3

I attended Tsing Hua University, where I majored in Electronics and Communication Engineering. My hobbies include playing basketball, reading novels and hiking. I'm an easy-going person who works well with everyone. I enjoy being around different types of people, and I always like to challenge myself to improve everything I do.

我曾在清華大學主修電子通訊工程專業。我愛好打籃球、閱讀小說和健行。我為人隨和，與人合作愉快。我喜歡與不同的人相處，我總是不斷挑戰自己，努力完善所做的每一件事。

Answer 4

I went to Tsing Hua University, where I majored in Electronics & Communication Engineering. Afterwards, I started my career at this company as a software engineer. I've been here for 3 years. I love solving riddles and puzzles, and I also enjoy jogging, reading and watching movies.

我曾就讀於清華大學，主修電子通訊工程專業。之後，我在現在的公司做軟體工程師，開始了我的職業生涯。至今我已工作了三年。我喜歡解謎、玩拼圖，我也愛好慢跑、讀書和看電影。

>> **Q2　What are your greatest strengths?**
　　談談你的優點。　　track 002

　　這是一個常見的問題。為什麼面試官要這麼問呢？因為面試官想要知道一旦他雇用你之後，能不能藉由你的優點為公司帶來利

益。優點包括你的工作技能、具有的各類證書和實際經驗，HR想要聽的優點不見得是你最凸出的優點，而是和你應徵的工作相關之優點，從中找出雇用你的理由，同時可以知道你對自己的了解程度，看看你對自己有沒有信心，以及你到底適合不適合這份工作。因此，你要精確地描述，不可泛泛地說一些無意義的話，例如，適應力強、具有幽默感、合群等等。

Answer 1

My greatest strength is to be assertive, and to express myself in written and oral communication. If there are problems, I'm good at talking them out in a calm and kind manner.

我最大的長處是堅定，而且能夠用書面和口語溝通表達自己。如果有問題存在的話，我善於冷靜而友善地用談話來解決。

Answer 2

My greatest strength is that I'm a hard and careful worker, and I have the ability to learn anything easily.

我最大的優點是勤奮而且細心，我能輕鬆地學習新事物。

Answer 3

I understand that every company has a different expectation of each employee. I think I am good at responding and adjusting to those needs.

我知道每個公司對於不同的員工有不同的要求。我認為我很擅長回應並調整自己以滿足那些要求。

Answer 4

My greatest strength is my confidence. I've learned to love myself for who I am, and that shows in my personality and my everyday attitude. I have grown to be a very positive and optimistic person.

我最大的長處在於我的自信。我學會愛自己的特質個性，還有自己的生活態度。我是一個十分正面樂觀的人。

Answer 5

When I'm working on a project, I don't want just to meet deadlines. Rather, I prefer to complete the project well ahead of schedule.

當我處理一項工作專案時，我想要做的不僅是在按時完成。更確切地說，我更想要提前完美地完成任務。

Answer 6

I have exceeded my sales goals every quarter, and I've earned a bonus each year since I started with my current employer.

我每一季都能超額完成銷售目標，從我開始目前的工作起，每年都能拿到獎金。

Answer 7

My time management skills are excellent, and I'm organized and efficient. I take pride in excelling at my work.

我善於管理時間，我做事有條理、效率高。我對我的工作很擅長，這令我很自豪。

Answer 8

I pride myself on my customer service skills and my ability to resolve what could be difficult situations.

我以我的客戶服務能力為豪，並且我解決難題和困境的能力也很棒。

>> **Q3   What are your greatest weaknesses?**
    談談你的缺點。 track 003

　　在求職面試中，往往要求列舉求職者的一些缺點。被問到這樣的問題時，需要注意以下幾點。

1. 不宜說自己沒缺點。
2. 不宜把明顯的優點說成缺點。
3. 不宜說出嚴重影響所應徵工作的缺點。
4. 不宜說出令人不放心、不舒服的缺點。
5. 可以說一些對於所應徵工作「無關緊要」的缺點，甚至是一些表面上看是缺點，從工作的角度看卻是優點的缺點。

Answer 1

Being organized wasn't my strongest point, but I implemented a time management system that really helped my organization skills.

做事有條理不是我的強項，但我實施了一項時間管理方案，真的幫助我提高了做事的條理性。

Answer 2

I like to make sure that my work is perfect, so sometimes I spend a little too much time checking it. However, I've

Chapter 2

come to a good balance by setting up a system to ensure everything is done correctly the first time.

我總是想要使得工作趨於完美，所以有時花了比較多的時間檢查。然而，我已經找到了一個平衡，透過建立一個系統確保所有事在一開始就全部正確執行。

Answer 3

I used to wait until the last minute to set appointments for the coming week, but I have realized that scheduling in advance makes much more sense.

以前我總是不到最後一刻不做下一周的計畫，但我現在意識到提前做計畫才能更有意義。

Answer 4

I would say that I can be too much of a perfectionist in my work. Sometimes I spend more time than necessary on a task, or take on tasks personally that could easily be delegated to someone else. Although I've never missed a deadline, it is still an effort for me to know when to move on to the next task, and to be confident when assigning work to others.

我想說我在工作中過於追求完美。有時候，我在一項任務上花費時間過多，或者將一些可以分配給別人的任務自己一個人攬下來。雖然我都按時完成任務了，但我仍需努力，以便決定何時開始下一項任務，以及更為自信地將工作分配給其他人。

Chapter 2

Answer 5

I used to like to work on one project to its completion before starting another, but I've learned to work on many projects at the same time. I think it allows me to be more creative and effective in each one.

過去我總是只能集中於一個任務，直到完成才能開始下一個，但現在我學會了同時進行多個任務。我覺得這使得我更富有創造力了，而且在每一個任務上的效率也提高了。

Answer 6

My greatest weakness is being shy. I tend to be shy when I meet new people, but when I get better acquainted with them, things usually work out well. Also, when I raise a new idea that I'm scared others won't buy, I get nervous that it won't go well. But once I start to work on the idea, I won't stop until it's accomplished. I usually get good feedback afterwards.

我最大的缺點就是害羞。我與陌生人相處時就容易害羞，但一旦熟悉之後，狀況就會好轉。另外，當我提出新主意時，我總是怕別人不贊同我，我會緊張事情不順利。但我一旦開始為主意付出行動時，我就不會放棄，直到完成。之後我通常能得到好的反饋。

Answer 7

I don't have enough courage to speak many words, due to my speech impairment. I realized that I need to talk to someone in order to get my thoughts across, and practice to make it better.

由於我的語言障礙，我總是沒有足夠的勇氣說很多話。我意識到我需要與人交流來讓人了解我的想法，練習才能變得更好。

Answer 8

My weakness is that I always put new things and new ideas at work, even when I know that some colleagues are happy to do it the way they used to. Sometimes people do not like this.

我的缺點就是我在工作時總是喜歡嘗試新的事物、新的觀念，但我知道同事喜歡用他們所習慣的傳統方式來做。有時大家不是很喜歡我的這個特點。

≫ Q4　How would your friends and colleagues describe you?
你的朋友和同事怎樣描述你？　 track 004

　　這個問題本質上還是對個人性格、品質和能力的詢問，只是採用了更為客觀的問題形式。在被問到這樣的問題時，基本原則與上述的自我介紹、談談優缺點等問題是相似的。還要注意，這樣的問題形式往往會讓應徵者以更為謙虛的方式回答，這時應仍保持自信，並以專業、簡潔，並且真實的方式回答。

Answer 1

Colleagues who worked close to me can tell that I am a good listener and always go the extra mile to help out others.

和我關係親密的同事認為我是個很好的聽眾，總是竭盡所能幫助

他人。

Answer 2

Colleagues from my team can tell that I am a cooperative, honest, and empathetic person, and loyal to my friends.

和我一組的同事認為我是個善於合作、誠實、具有同情心的人，並且忠於我的朋友。

Answer 3

People who I supervise would describe me as a coacher, and a strong advocator for their good performance.

我管理過的人覺得我是個很好的指導者，是鼓勵他們取得好業績的宣導者。

Answer 4

People who I supervise would describe me as a dream chaser and a person who they are ready to follow.

我管理過的人覺得我是個追夢者，是他們可以跟隨的。

Answer 5

My co-workers would describe me as a hard worker and a quick learner.

我的同事認為我是個工作勤奮，學習能力強的人。

Answer 6

My friends would describe me as a good planner and a determined professional.

我的朋友認為我是個擅長計畫的人，並且是位意志堅定的專家。

>> Q5 Do you prefer working in a team environment or by yourself?
與人合作或獨自工作？ track 005

　　這個問題事實上是對你的合作能力和獨立工作能力的考察。而不是真正問你願意和別人一起工作還是自己一個人工作。因此，被問到這個問題時，應分別展現<u>自己與人合作的能力</u>，以及<u>獨自工作的能力</u>。

Answer 1

I have worked on teams and independently as well. Some jobs require a teamwork effort, while others fit individual work.

我既與別人合作過也單獨工作過。有的工作適合團隊合作，而有的工作適合單獨工作。

Answer 2

Though I prefer to work alone, I am a great team player. Working with others has taught me how to avoid conflict, and make compromises. I think my team playing ability is in balance with my individual performance.

雖然我比較喜歡單獨工作，我也是很有團隊精神的。與他人合作教會我如何避免爭端，達成妥協。我覺得我的團隊合作能力和獨自工作表現一樣可圈可點。

Answer 3

In my previous jobs, I have had opportunities to work in a team on an impromptu basis, as well as provide technical support to the product that is being developed by the team. I have immensely enjoyed playing both roles, and I think that I would be comfortable in both roles, that of a team member as well as a sole entity.

之前的工作中，我曾有機會與他人暫時進行團隊合作，同時我也為團隊研發的產品提供技術支援。我非常享受同時扮演兩個角色，我覺得兩種角色對我而言都相當輕鬆，作為一個團隊成員或是單獨的個體。

Answer 4

I find that working in a team increases my work performance, and also creates a proper work flow and information distribution between team members. This can help to complete a project in a timely and efficient manner. While working independently, I realized that I was the complete owner of the project and considered this responsibility as an incentive. Therefore, I have had very good experiences working in a team, as well as working independently.

我發現團隊合作可以提升我的工作業績，也能在組員之間制訂出一個合適的工作流程和資訊分配路徑。這可以幫助準時有效率地完成一個計畫。而獨自工作時，我自己就是一個項目的完全掌控者，我將這種責任當成是一種激勵。因此，我既有豐富的團隊合作經驗，也有獨自工作經驗。

>> Q6 Tell me about your family.
談談你的家庭。 track 006

　　這個問題對於了解應徵者的性格、觀念、心態等有一定的作用，這是招聘單位問該問題的主要原因。對於這樣的問題，回答時，一般先簡單地介紹家庭成員，適度地強調溫馨和睦的家庭氣氛，強調父母對自己教育的重視，強調每一位家庭成員的良好狀況、大家對自己工作的支持，以及自己對家庭的責任感。

Answer 1

My family is not big. We are three altogether — my mother, my wife, and I. My father passed away a few years ago. My mother is fifty-seven years old. She is a retired worker. My wife is a nurse and she is pregnant.

我家人口不多。總共三口人——我媽媽，我妻子和我。我爸爸幾年前去世了。我媽媽今年57歲，是個退休勞工，我妻子是個護士，她現在懷孕了。

Answer 2

There are five people in my family, including my grandmother, my parents, my elder brother and myself. My father is an engineer, and my mother is a housewife. My brother is a journalist. He is still a happy single man like me. We live a happy life together.

我家有五口人，包括我奶奶、我父母親、我哥哥和我自己。我父親是個工程師，我母親是個家庭主婦。我哥哥是個記者，他跟我一樣，仍然是個快活的單身漢。我們一家在一起過著幸福的生活。

Answer 3

People say there is a generation gap in the world today, but I don't think there is one in my family. Meals are very lively at our house. I often watch TV together with my family in the evenings. On weekends or holidays, we sometimes go to parks, cinemas, and concerts together.

人們說今天這個世界有代溝，但是我認為我們家沒有代溝。吃飯在我們家是很熱鬧的。晚上我經常和家人在一起看電視。週末和假日我們有時一起去公園、看電影、聽音樂會。

Answer 4

I get along well with my sister. She is preparing for college entrance exams right now, so she asks me for advice a lot. We often go swimming and shopping together on weekends.

我和妹妹相處得很好。她現在正在準備大學入學考試，所以經常向我請教。我們週末經常一起去游泳和購物。

▶▶ Q7   How do you spend your leisure time?
你有什麼業餘愛好？ track 007

　　業餘愛好能在一定程度上反映應徵者的性格、觀念、心態等，記得不要說自己有哪些庸俗的、令人感覺不好的愛好；也別說自己僅限於讀書、聽音樂、上網，否則可能令面試官懷疑應徵者性格孤僻、太宅，最好能有一些戶外的業餘愛好來「點綴」你的形象。

Answer 1

I like to play football and basketball with my friends. I can surely say I am a team player who is driven by targets. Further, I am pretty aggressive in achieving results on a team.

我喜歡和朋友踢足球、打籃球。我敢保證我是個有明確目標、善於合作的人。此外，在達成團隊比賽分數時，我非常地積極。

Answer 2

I often play Sudoku puzzles alone during my leisure time. Recently, I've taken a piano course for beginners. I also made friends with my piano-course classmates.

閒暇時，我經常一個人玩數獨。最近我報了個鋼琴基礎班，並且和鋼琴班的同學成了朋友。

Answer 3

I like to go hiking. I work hard and usually don't take a break at my desk, so weekends are time for me to keep fit. There are some nice hills around my apartment worth walking around. Recently, I have been getting into photography, but mostly outdoors and scenery.

我喜歡健行。我努力工作，工作時基本都不會休息，所以週末就是我運動的時間。在我公寓附近有些漂亮的小山值得走走逛逛。最近我喜歡上拍照，但是拍的大都是戶外和風景。

Answer 4

I really enjoy doing yoga. I can hold a yoga pose for a long period of time with some slow music. During that time I can do some meditating, which helps me figure things out. And in summer, I go fishing with my dad very often. Therefore, a job that requires a lot of patience or focus could fit me well.

我很喜歡練瑜伽。在輕音樂中，我可以保持一個瑜伽姿勢很長時間。同時我也會做些冥想，這樣可以幫助我思考問題。夏天時，我常和爸爸去釣魚。所以一個需要耐心和集中力的工作非常適合我。

》》Q8　Who do you admire?
　　你崇拜誰？  track 008

　　HR往往會用這個問題來進一步挖掘應徵者的性格和價值觀等。你所崇拜的人所擁有的特質往往也是你所重視並努力擁有的。在回答這個問題時，要與你所應徵的職位相聯繫起來，也就是你所應徵的職位需要具有什麼樣特質的人才，你所崇拜的人就應儘量擁有這樣的特質，這樣才能使得用人單位認為你就是他們要找的人，就是適合這份工作的人。

Answer 1

My hero is my father. He taught me to do the right thing, to value others and to help them whenever I can. I also learned to plan ahead, to work hard, and to do my best in any situation. Dad tought me to be a lifelong learner, to smile and keep a sense of humor even when things get tough, and to love, support and protect my family.

我崇拜的人是我的父親。他教導我要做善事、珍惜他人、當我有能力時要幫助別人。我也學到要提前準備、努力工作、無論何時都要盡力做到最好。父親教我要終身學習、保持微笑、就算遇到難題也要保持幽默感、要愛家、養家、顧家。

Answer 2

I admire my mother the most. She knows how to value people and help them as far as she can. She plans ahead, works hard and gives her best shot in any situation. She believes anything can be achieved if the intent to do it and the willingness to learn is there.

我最崇拜媽媽。她知道如何衡量一個人的價值，並竭盡所能幫助他人。她計畫在先，努力工作，任何情況下都盡力做到最好。她認為凡事皆有可能，只要有想做的決心和想學的意願。

Answer 3

I have always been inspired by the legendary Greek hero *Leonidous*. He knew that he faced grave dangers and could have lost his life, but for his countrymen he took the giant leap.

我一直都很崇拜極具傳奇色彩的希臘英雄萊奧尼達斯。他明知面臨危險，可能會喪命，可是為了他的人民，他堅持作戰，壯烈犧牲。

Answer 4

I admire the proactive persistence of *Thomas Edison*. He remained persistent, even after many failed attempts, because he never ran out of ideas. *Thomas Edison* didn't stop at 3 alternatives, or 4 or 5. He didn't even stop at 10,000. When he reached experiment 9,999 he was asked by a reporter, "Sir, are you going to fail 10,000 times?" *Edison* confidently replied, "I have not failed at each attempt; rather I've succeeded at discovering another way not to invent an electric lamp."

我很仰慕*湯瑪斯愛迪生*的堅持不懈。不管失敗多少次，他都堅持做實驗，因為他不斷有新想法。*愛迪生*沒有在第三次嘗試後就放棄，第四次、第五次也沒有放棄。即使是1萬次也沒有放棄。當他的實驗進行到第9,999次時，有記者問他，「先生，你是準備失敗1萬次嗎？」*愛迪生*非常自信地回答：「我的每次嘗試不是失敗，而是成功地發現了另一個不能發明電燈的方法。」

Chapter 2

date:　　　／　／

📁 Q&A Time—About the Past 關於過去

>> **Q1 Why were you fired?**
你為什麼被開除？ track 009

　　這個問題較為尖銳，一般理解為被迫離開上一個單位。在回答這個問題時，要注意，首先不能把這個問題看成是一個承認錯誤的機會。也就是說，要表明「被開除錯不在我」。但同時也要注意，不要指責以前的老闆或是同事，這無疑會給面試官留下不好的印象，也會讓面試官懷疑你所說的話的真實性。

Answer 1

The broad-based restructuring at my former company resulted in my position being eliminated. However, during my time there I was successful at my job as a department director. I worked very hard and got along well with my colleagues. Now I'm excited about having the opportunity to meet new challenges.

因為前公司大規模的組織重組，我的職位被取消了。但是在我任職期間，作為一個部門經理我很成功。我努力工作，與同事關係很好。現在我很期待有機會能迎接新挑戰。

Answer 2

A new manager came in and cleaned house in order to bring in members of his old team. I outlasted several downsizings, but the last one included me. Sign of the times,

I guess. It was the manager's right, but it cleared my head to envision better opportunities elsewhere. The opportunity we're discussing seems to be made for me, and I hope to eventually grow into a position of responsibility.

公司來了一個新的經理，為了把他以前的團隊帶進來，所以要裁員。我躲過了好幾次裁員，但是沒躲過最後一次。我猜，這也是一種時代的終結吧。新任經理有權利裁員，但是我也對未來的工作機會進行了展望。現在我們正在討論的這個工作機會就像是為我量身訂製的，我希望您能給我機會挑起這份責任。

Answer 3

Although circumstances caused me to leave my last job, I was very successful in school and got along well with both students and faculty. Perhaps I didn't fully understand my boss's expectations. I certainly don't know why he released me before I had a chance to prove myself. Being cut loose was a blessing in disguise, though. Now I have an opportunity to explore jobs that better suit my qualifications and interests.

雖然因為某些原因導致我離職，但是我讀書時和老師同學相處得都還不錯。也許是我沒有充分理解老闆的期待。我真的不知道為什麼他在我還沒有充分表現自己時就解雇了我。然而被解雇也不一定是壞事。現在我有機會尋找更符合我的專業和興趣的工作。

Answer 4

My boss and I were unable to work effectively together. I have thought about this a great deal, and I can understand now what went wrong. I did not have a clear understanding of the task expectations. I should have asked for further clarification. I have learned from this, and I am positive about being able to make a valuable contribution to this organization.

我和我老闆無法有效率地合作。關於這件事，我思考了很多，現在我終於明白到底是哪裡出了錯。我並沒有很好地理解工作任務的期待。我應該請求更詳細的解釋。我從這件事中學到教訓，現在我很期待可以在這個組織做出有價值的貢獻。

Answer 5

Certain personal problems, which I now have solved, unfortunately upset my work life. But that job was a learning experience, and I think I'm wiser now. These problems no longer exist, and I'm up and running strong to exceed expectations in my new job. I'd like the chance to prove that to you.

因為一些個人原因我被解雇了，但是這些原因我都已經解決了，雖然是賠上了我的工作。我的上一份工作是一份經驗教訓，我覺得我現在更加睿智了。現在問題不復存在，我已經準備好在新工作中超越期待，希望您能給我機會。

Answer 6

My competencies were not the right match for my previous employer's needs, but it looks like they'd be a good fit in your organization. I have discovered so much about myself and developed a number of skills dealing with all the challenges I faced. In addition to marketing and advertising, I believe skills in promotion will be valued here.

我的能力並不太符合上一任雇主的需求，但是貌似很適合貴公司。在過去面臨的挑戰中，我對自己有了更多的了解，也培養了不少技能。除了市場行銷和廣告業務，我相信這裡需要宣傳促銷這技能。

▶▶ Q2　Why did you leave your last job？
你為什麼離職呢？　 track 010

　　這個問題與上一個問題相似，但語氣緩和許多，可以理解為離職是應徵者自己的主動行為。因此在回答上相對容易一些，但也有一定的技巧。離職的原因不能給面試官留下你在他的公司也不會長久工作的印象。一般來說，有尋求發展機會、渴望挑戰、工作地點不滿意等原因，具體回答技巧如下。

Answer 1

I was desperate for work and took the wrong job without looking around the corner. I won't make that mistake again. I'd prefer an environment that is congenial, structured and team-oriented, where my best talents can shine and I can make a substantial contribution.

我之前太急於找工作了，所以沒了解具體情況就接手了並不適合我的工作。我不會再犯同樣的錯了。我更喜歡一個志趣相投、有組織的、重視團隊合作的環境，在這樣的環境中，我可發揮潛能，我能做出實際貢獻。

Answer 2

There was a great deal of uncertainty about the security of my previous job. I am looking for a stable company where there is a long-term opportunity to grow and advance.

我的上一份工作充滿了太多的不確定性。我希望能在一個穩定的公司,找到一份長期的工作,謀求發展與突破。

Answer 3

I have reached the ceiling in my particular job, and I am ready for more responsibility. I am interested in an opportunity to use the skills and abilities I have developed over the last couple of years in a new and challenging position.

我覺得我在之前的工作中已經達到頂峰,我已經準備好挑起更多責任。對於在一個全新的、具有挑戰性的職位上,發揮我在過去幾年中培養出來的技能,我非常感興趣。

Answer 4

After a number of years in my last position, I believed that I had reached the ceiling. I needed to make a career move. I am now looking for a new experience where I can contribute and grow in a bigger environment.

在舊職位多年後,我覺得我已經達到頂峰,我需要來一次職業轉型。我正在尋找一種新的體驗,能讓我在更寬廣的環境中發展並做出貢獻。

Answer 5

In all honesty, I wasn't really looking to move jobs, but this looks like such a great opportunity to use my skills and experience. I have always admired this company.

說實話，我並沒有考慮過換工作，但是這次的機會非常有利於我發揮我的技能和經驗。我一直很敬仰貴公司。

Answer 6

I recently received my degree, and I want to utilize my educational background in my next position.

我最近剛獲得了新學位，我希望能在下一份工作中利用我的教育背景。

Answer 7

I was spending hours each day commuting. I would prefer to be closer to home.

我每天上下班都要花費數小時，我希望離家近一點。

Answer 8

I am relocating to this area for family reasons and left my job to make this move.

我遷至此地是由於我的家庭原因，所以我辭去上一份工作。

》》Q3 What didn't you like about your previous job?
　　　　你對你上一份工作有什麼不滿意的地方？　🔘 track 011

　　這個問題有如一個陷阱。事實上，HR是想看你對他們正在招人的這份工作會不會滿意。如果這份工作的情況和你上一份工作類

似，而你對上一份工作不滿意的話，很有可能對這份工作也不會滿意。因此，回答這個問題時，要特別留意，回答要有技巧。

Answer 1

There was a lack of growth opportunities, as the company was quite small. One of the reasons I am so interested in your company is that it is a much bigger organization with formal career planning structures in place.

公司規模太小所以缺少成長空間。我對貴公司感興趣的願意之一就是，貴公司是一個規模較大的公司，並且有職涯規劃體系。

Answer 2

There was very little opportunity for me to use my initiative. I regard this as one of my strengths; I found it frustrating that I was unable to get past the bureaucracy of such a big company to implement any improvements. That is why I am enthusiastic about working for a smaller company like this one, which I know will encourage employees to use their initiative.

過去（在那裡）很少有機會能讓我運用自己的自主能力。我將這種能力視為我的優勢之一；我發現在大公司，我根本無法與官僚主義抗衡為公司做出貢獻時，我很失望。這就是為什麼我希望在一個像貴公司這樣較小型的公司工作的原因，因為規模較小的公司都鼓勵員工發揮他們的自主能力。

Answer 3

I've given this question some thought, and overall I've been very satisfied with my jobs. I've been able to work with some really interesting people. But I have to say that I did have a job where there was an inordinate amount of paperwork. Because working with people is my strength, the paperwork really bogged me down at times.

針對這個問題，我思考過很多次，整體來說，我很滿意我之前的工作。我可以和一些很有趣的人一起工作，但是我必須要說，我工作中的文書工作實在是多得不合常理。與人打交道是我的特長，但是文書工作常常讓我陷入僵局。

Answer 4

As a fresh face in the working world, the company offers a great opportunity for a good entry level position. However, after being there for so many years, I felt I was not able to reach my full potential because of the lack of challenges. I also didn't think there was room for advancement in the company. I did enjoy working there and appreciate the skills I developed while with the company. But I feel my skill set can be better utilized elsewhere, where my capabilities are more recognized and there is the opportunity for growth.

作為一個職場新人，公司提供了很多適合剛入門的人的工作機會。但是工作這麼多年後，我發現我沒法充分發揮我的潛能，因為缺少挑戰。我也不認為公司有上升空間。我喜歡在那裡工作，我也很感激在那裡學到的技能。但是我覺得我的技能在別處能得到更好地利用，同時我的能力也會更受賞識，我也更有成長空間。

›› Q4　What did you like about your previous job?
你對先前工作的滿意之處是什麼？ track 012

　　除了提問關於對先前工作的不滿之處，面試官還可能問到你對其滿意的地方。這時，你應找出先前工作的優點加以點評。一般來說，可以提及像是「有很好的發展空間」、「有很多學習的機會」或是「有和諧的工作環境」等，以表明自己是一個有進取心，以及喜歡和同事們和諧相處的人。當然，不要過於誇耀前一個工作，這只會讓面試官認為你更換工作的意願並不那麼強烈。

Answer 1

I liked the professional attitude and the workplace environment that was provided for me. I enjoyed having to use my initiative. I implemented and improved a number of systems, including the order processing system.

我喜歡公司專業的工作態度和提供給我的工作環境。我很樂於運用自己的自主能力。我補充並改進了很多系統，包括訂單處理系統。

Answer 2

I loved my boss, who recently retired. He was a terrific guy to work for, and I'll miss working for him. I enjoyed the people I worked with and felt I was very productive. It was a friendly and fun atmosphere, and I actually enjoyed going into work each morning.

我喜歡我的老闆，他最近剛退休。他是個很值得為其工作的人，我很懷念為他工作的日子。我很喜歡與我一起共事的人，他們讓我覺得自己很有效率。工作氣氛很和樂而且有趣，每天去上班我都很開心。

Answer 3

I felt the leadership team was great. They knew all of their employees on a first-name basis and tried to make personal connections. I also enjoyed the fact that the office tried to do community outreach with local organizations.

我覺得領導團體很棒。他們知道每個員工的名字，並且嘗試建立私人聯繫。他們也試著與當地的各種組織合作，組織社區服務活動。

Answer 4

I appreciated the close-knit interpersonal communications between managers and employees. The company believed in their employees and seemed to really think about my future growth and professional progress. The company constantly asked for feedback to improve job performance and to help achieve corporate goals.

我很滿意管理人員和員工之間的組織嚴密性和人際交流。公司很相信員工，而且似乎真的考慮到我將來的成長和專業上的進步。公司會不斷地徵求回饋以提高工作品質並協助達到公司目標。

>> **Q5　What were your responsibilities?**
　　你工作的職責是什麼？ track 013

　　在問這個問題時，面試官真正關心的不是你以前工作是做什麼的，而是由你以前的工作職責來判斷你是否能勝任當下的職位。因此，回答這個問題時，要與眼前應徵職位的職責相聯繫起來，找一些有關聯的部分說，而不要說一些風馬牛不相及的內容，即使那真的是你曾經工作的職責，也不是面試官所關心的部分。

Chapter 2

Answer 1

My top three responsibilities were to account for all cash, checks, and credit card receipts at the end of my shift and balance those with what our management information system calculated. I was responsible for auditing the cycle counts of all merchandise in my area, and I also trained newcomers to the company.

我最主要的三個工作職責是在交接工作時，解釋現金、支票和信用卡收入，並且與管理資訊系統的計算結果相符合。我負責審計所有在我的區域內的商品迴圈計數，我還負責培訓公司的新人。

Answer 2

Working as a secretary, I make professional phone calls to clients and customers, answer the phone, and transfer calls. Providing information about the business to clients and customers is also one of my responsibilities. I'm able to use the computer, copy machine, and other office equipment. I also need to write letters and schedule meetings for my boss.

作為一名秘書，我打電話給客戶和顧客、接聽電話，以及轉接電話。為客戶和顧客提供業務資訊也是我的職責之一。我會使用電腦、影印機等各種辦公設備。我也需要為我的老闆寫信，以及安排會議。

Answer 3

I am a public relations coordinator with five years of

experience in this field. I am responsible for managing effectively the communications of our clients, including press releases, presentations, and speeches. I also coordinate events, conduct market research, and create marketing or communication plans in both English and French. Being extroverted, a team player, and a leader at the same time have made me successful at what I do.

我在這一行做了五年公關。我負責有效率地管理與客戶間的溝通，做新聞發布、簡報、演講。我也用英語和法語協調事件、組織市場調查、製作行銷或者交流方案。我很外向、善於團隊合作，以及領導他人，所以作為一個公關我很成功。

Answer 4

As a sales manager, I'm responsible for directing our company's sales program. I usually assign sales territories, set goals, and establish training programs for our sales representatives. I also advise our sales representatives on ways to improve their sales performance, achieve goals and obtain expected quotas.

作為一個業務經理，我的職責是管理我們公司的銷售專案。我經常給我們的業務代表分配業務區域、設定銷售目標，以及設立培訓專案。我也會針對如何提高銷售業績、完成銷售目標、達到期望值這些問題給我們的業務代表提出建議。

Chapter 2

▶▶ Q6　How would you describe your boss?
描述一下你的老闆。　 track 014

　　面試中常見的問題還有「描述一下你的老闆。」這樣的問題回答起來往往也很需要技巧。首先不能說過去的老闆是「完美的老闆」，這無疑會給面試官，也就是將來可能成為你老闆的人留下不好的印象。其次，不要說對過去老闆的不滿之處。最後，不要有不實之言。

Answer 1

My manager had a good combination of professionalism and the personal touch. Having risen from an entry-level employee, he knew most of the problems that employees faced. He was a good leader and had strong communication skills.

我的上司工作專業，為人親切。他是從底層員工做起的，所以他清楚地知道員工面臨的問題。他是個很棒的領導者，有著很出色的溝通能力。

Answer 2

I've learned a lot from my boss. He motivated me to come up with new ideas and always provided helpful feedback. He always set, changed, evaluated and monitored our work goals to improve our bottom line.

我的老闆教會了我很多。他總是激勵我多想一些新主意，並且總是給我很有幫助的回饋。他總是設定、修改、評價、並且監督我們的工作目標，以提高我們的底線目標。

Chapter 2

Answer 3

My manager was very experienced. He had managed a number of large programs in the preceding 8 years. He liked his staff to be able to work independently, and I had to learn quickly to become independent while analyzing problems and finding solutions.

我的經理很有經驗，過去八年間，他接手過很多大型計畫。他希望他的員工可以獨立工作，所以我必須在分析問題、找出解決問題的方案時，快速學習、變得獨立。

Answer 4

My last boss was terrific. He was very creative and offered opportunities to improve my learning. He always made time to listen to employee concerns and was a strong leader. There was a high level of trust between us, and each of us knew what to expect from the other.

我的上一任老闆很棒。他很有創造力，並且提供機會提高我的學習能力。他總是擠出時間傾聽員工的擔憂，是個強大的領導者。我們彼此信任度很高，並且也相互知曉對方的能力。

》 Q7 When was the last time you were angry? What happened?

你上一次生氣是什麼時候？發生了什麼？ track 015

生氣意味著發洩，也就是一個人的情緒在某種程度上不受控制。面試官問這個問題主要是想看應徵者控制情緒的能力以及其不

能控制自我情緒的點在何處。回答這個問題時，一般首先表明自己是一個很善於控制自我情緒的人，一般情況下不會生氣或發火。其次，可以用「當我知道我能做到而沒有做好的時候我會生氣。」等答案來藉這個問題進一步凸顯自己的一些優點，例如負責、關心工作等。

Answer 1

I'm good at working on a team, but it can be frustrating when people did not cooperate. But I never get angry with my team members.

我的團隊合作能力很棒，但如果大家不配合的話，我會有些低落。但我從不會對我的隊友生氣。

Answer 2

Anger to me means loss of control. I do not lose control. When I get stressed, I step back, take a deep breath, thoughtfully think through the situation, and then begin to formulate a plan of action.

對於我來說，生氣就是失去控制。我不會失去控制。當我感到有壓力的時候，我就退一步、深呼吸，好好地思考當時的狀況，然後開始計畫下一步該怎麼做。

Answer 3

I don't remember when the last time was. Anger is something I have learned to control over time. When I am about to get angry, I simply take a step back, take a deep breath, drink a bit of water, and I am fine thereafter.

我不記得上次生氣是什麼時候了。憤怒已經是一種我能掌握的情感。當我快要生氣時，我會退後一步、深呼吸、喝點水，然後我就好了。

Answer 4

Our lives are not only determined by what happens to us, but by how we react to what happens. I think being angry is totally wrong. I don't want to be a loser, and I've learned how to control my anger.

我們的生活並不是由發生的事決定，而是由我們對事件的反應決定。我認為生氣完全是不對的。我不想成為生活的輸家，我已經學會如何控制憤怒。

>> **Q8 What is the most difficult situation you have faced in a workplace?**
你工作時遇到的最大的難題是什麼？ track 016

　　面試官提出這個問題主要是想看應徵者解決問題的能力。在面試前，先想好幾個自己曾經在工作中遇到的難題，以及解決的方法。回答這個問題時，應展現自己能夠隨機應變，並有臨危不亂處理問題的能力。一般來說，回答分為四個部分，一是對難題的描述，二是處理方法，三是這樣處理的理由，四是處理的結果。

Answer 1

One of our team members left us because we couldn't reach an agreement on the task we were running. Even though it

Chapter 2

was difficult when she quit without notice, we still managed to rearrange the department workload to cover the position until a replacement was hired. Everyone was very busy then, but somehow it helped strengthen our abilities.

因為正在進行的任務無法達成一致意見，我們的一位組員離開了我們。雖然她的突然離開給我們造成很大困難，但是我們仍然成功地重新分配了部門工作量，並且堅持到空缺被填補上。那時每個人都很忙，但是這反而協助鍛鍊了我們的能力。

Answer 2

Once, we were faced with a sudden order increase for our new product. It was for a new customer. I immediately sat down with the production supervisor, our materials manager, and the union steward. We were able to lay out a workable plan that maximized hourly labor costs, guaranteed materials were available and, with only a slight adjustment, met the production deadline. While it was challenging and involved long hours, the pay-off was a signed contract with a new customer.

有一次我們遇到了新產品突然增加訂單，是一位新客戶。我立刻與生產主任、材料經理、工會代表開會協商。我們制定出了一個可行方案，最大化每小時的勞動量，保證材料供應，而且僅僅用了一個微小的調整，我們就趕上了交貨日期。這件事很具挑戰性，投入了大量的時間，但是回報很豐厚，我們與新客戶簽訂了合約。

Answer 3

When I was working on a software implementation team, we

took over another company and had to transit many clients to a new product in a short amount of time. It took a lot of planning, time, hard work, and effort, but we were able to complete the project in a timely manner.

當我在一個軟體安裝小組工作時，我們取代了另一家公司，所以必須要在短時間內將大量客戶轉移到新產品。我們做了很多計畫、花了很多時間、投入很多精力，但最終我們及時完成了這個專案。

Answer 4

My department manager asked me to investigate a bottleneck in the production line. I did some research and suggested a redesign of the department layout so that the production units were in a more efficient sequence. It worked so well, increasing production by up to 20 percent, that my layout design has been adopted by all our branches.

我的部門經理讓我去調查生產線的瓶頸問題。我做了一些研究，建議重新設計一下部門的格局安排，這樣各個生產單位的排列順序就會更有效率。結果很不錯，提高了20%的生產率，並且我的格局布置已經被所有分公司採納。

>> **Q9 What was your greatest achievement at your previous job?**
你在之前的工作中最大的成就是什麼？ track 017

　　當被問到這個問題的時候，應徵者應該從專業的角度去回答在上一個工作中對所在職位和單位所做出的貢獻，而不是從個人的角度去回答。這是一個很好的展現專業技能和個人能力的機會，應好好利用。

Answer 1

One time, a new software development project was running behind. I took the initiative and interacted with the team members. We successfully started its development, solved the issues, and delivered it on time.

有一次，一個開發軟體的新專案有點耽擱。我積極主動地與團隊成員溝通。我們成功地啟動專案、解決問題並且準時提交。

Answer 2

My greatest achievement would likely be when I was able to complete the entire year's worth of tax calculations, including extra quality checks, a full month before deadline. It freed up time to get started on the next year's balances and saved the company roughly $50,000 in excess work.

我最大的成就是我完成了全年的稅務計算，整整提前了一個月，還包括外加的品質查核。這使得下一年的餘額計算時間變得寬鬆，為公司在多餘工作上節省了將近5萬美元。

Answer 3

We were on the verge of losing a client with whom we had been doing business for years. I discussed the problems with the customer. We changed our account handling procedures and were successful in keeping the business.

我們即將要失去一位已合作多年的老客戶。我與客戶仔細商談問題。我們改變了客戶處理的程序，然後成功地保住了這位客戶。

≫ Q10　Give us examples of teamwork in the workplace.
談談你的團隊工作經驗。　　track 018

公司裡的工作往往需要以團隊的形式進行，因此這個問題用來了解應徵者是否有較強的團隊合作能力，以評定應徵者是否適合此份工作。一般來說，在回答這個問題時，要儘量全面。也就是說，可以不用只說樂觀積極那方面，也可以說一些團隊工作中失敗的經驗，以及你們為此付出的努力，以顯示在團隊合作中得到的成長。最重要的是，展現自己的團隊合作能力。

Answer 1

As a project leader, I have had a variety of experiences dealing with project issues. Whenever I have faced a problem that requires a solution, I have collected data related to the issue, figured out the causes, and consulted with team members for solutions. When I have obtained neutral views of the issue, I have tried to resolve it in such a manner that I will continue keeping a keen eye on the solution and the betterment of the product.

作為一個專案領導者，我有很多處理問題的經驗。每當遇到問題，需要謀求解決方案時，我都會蒐集與問題相關的資訊，找出原因所在，並與組員探討解決方案。當對問題看法不確定時，我都會採取這種方式，並時刻關注解決方案和產品的改善。

Answer 2

In my last position, I was part of a software implementation team. We all worked together to plan and manage the implementation schedule, to provide customer training, and to ensure a smooth transition for our customers. Our team always completed our projects ahead of schedule, with very positive reviews from our clients.

我的上一份工作是在一個軟體安裝小組。我們一起組織計畫安裝的進程，提供客戶培訓，確保平穩的轉換過程。我們小組總是提前完成任務，客戶的回饋也很不錯。

Answer 3

I was part of a team responsible for evaluating and selecting a new vendor for our office equipment and supplies. The inter-departmental team reviewed options, compared pricing and service, chose a vendor, and implemented the transition to the new vendor.

我曾在一個團隊中，團隊的任務是評估選擇一個為我們提供辦公用品的新賣家。我們這個跨部門的團隊研究了各個選擇，對比價格和服務，選擇了新賣家，並成功地轉換到新賣家。

Answer 4

Our team was responsible for achieving the highest productivity for the company with the given resources. Therefore, we had to ensure that all the provided resources were at their optimum performance. We would hold meetings from time to time to ensure that any issues that our team members faced were resolved without any losses to either the company or the product that was being currently worked on.

我們團隊負責利用已有資源為公司完成最大的生產量。因此我們必須確保所有提供的資源都在最佳狀態。我們不時開會確認團隊成員遇到的問題都已經妥善解決，並且沒有對公司或正在生產的產品造成損失。

》 Q11　What have you done to develop your skills?
　　你是如何提高自己的能力的？　🔘 track 019

　　除了想了解應徵者所擁有的技能，面試官還會想探尋應徵者用來提高自己能力的途徑，來判斷應徵者是一個不斷學習、不斷進取的人，還是一個安於現狀的人。回答這個問題時，可以考慮從在理論中學習和在工作實踐中學習等方面入手。

Answer 1

I enrolled myself in a course in Visual Basic after work hours. The teacher of the course was very professional and experienced, and he really helped me a lot.

我在工作結束後去上一些有關Visual Basic的課程。授課老師很專業，也很有經驗，我受益匪淺。

Answer 2

I believe that learning is a continual process. With that in mind, I engaged myself in reading and surfing the net to explore new and bright ideas and re-create them, to help build a new system for myself.

我相信學習是個不間斷的過程。所以我堅持讀書、甚至上網來發現新穎的想法，並改進這些想法成為我自己的思想。

Chapter 2

Answer 3

I subscribed to job-related magazines for keeping me informed with newer studies in the subject.

我訂閱一些和工作相關的雜誌來讓自己隨時知道這個課題上的新研究。

Answer 4

I have always selected jobs that help me acquire new skills, to get an edge in software programming.

我選擇的工作，總是可以幫助我獲得新技能，在軟體設計方面得到優勢。

≫ Q12 Describe your communication skills.
描述一下你的溝通能力。 track 020

　　根據應徵職位的不同，有的需要很強的溝通能力，有的對溝通能力的要求並不是很高，但可以肯定的一點是，基本的溝通能力是必需的。遇到這個問題時，回想一下自己平日與同事、上司、客戶的溝通方式，並展現自己優秀的一面。同時，可以將這個問題與「團隊合作」相關問題聯繫起來，因為溝通能力需要被應用於團隊合作之中，而團隊合作也是很多工作所需要的。

Answer 1

I have had issues with peers, which is common in a professional workforce. However, I have always endeavored to solve the problems without the any repercussions. I always believe that conversation is the best way to solve any issues, and I have always had dialogues with any peer who has had an issue with me. I consider his/her point of view and the project goals before I take the conversation ahead.

我曾與同事有過爭論，在一個專業的工作團隊中這很常見。我一直盡力不留後患的解決問題。我相信對話是解決問題的最好方式，所以我總是跟與我有爭論的同事談話。在對話前，我會事先考慮他/她的觀點以及團隊目標。

Answer 2

When there are disagreements among my team members, I usually don't pay attention to the issue for the first few days. I have faith in the professionalism of my team partners. However, if the problem is not solved over a period of time, I make sure that I speak to any and all team members who are involved in the issue, to try to iron out an amicable solution with dialogue between them.

當團隊成員間有意見不一致時，通常一開始我並不會干涉。我相信團隊成員的專業精神。但是，如果一段時間後問題還是沒有解決，我會和每個相關的成員談話，試著通過談話找出妥善的解決方案。

Answer 3

I'm an extroverted person, so I always take the initiative to solve issues with my co-workers. I like to have an excellent professional relationship with my co-workers, which gells quite nicely with the company environment. People assist one another. We work as a team to solve problems and learn new skills to reach our team objectives.

我是個外向的人，所以我總是積極主動地解決與同事之間的問題。我喜歡和同事保持良好、專業的關係，這種關係與整個工作環境也很協調。大家互相支持，我們像一個團隊一樣在一起工作，解決問題、學習新技術來完成團隊目標。

Answer 4

For any disagreement between team members, I am the mediator. I will set a behavioral code if necessary. I believe that I should be a cohesive force between all the team members. I first get a lowdown on the actual problem and try to work out a solution to the conflict. Most conflicts can be worked out, if the right amount of time is given.

有任何爭端在團隊中發生時，我都是調停者。如果必要，我會設定行為準則。我確信我應該成為團隊成員間的粘合劑。我會先了解問題的實情，然後試著找出解決方案。如果有足夠的時間，大多數的爭端都能被解決。

≫ Q13 What do you think are the advantages and disadvantages of working in a team?
你認為團隊工作的優點和缺點是什麼？ track 021

　　無論哪一種工作，都會需要團隊合作。因此，求職面試中，關於團隊工作的問題也常常出現。面試官會以「你認為團隊工作的優點和缺點是什麼？」這樣的方式來考察應徵者的團隊工作能力和意向。

Chapter 2

Answer 1

There are many advantages of teamwork. As the old saying goes, "Two heads are better than one." Of course, with more minds set on a specific goal, you have access to more ideas. Looking at things from the perspective of others can increase the likelihood of quality innovation.

團隊合作有很多優點。有句老話叫做「三個臭皮匠勝過一個諸葛亮。」當然，愈多的人專注於一個目標，就愈能得到更多想法。從他人的角度看問題更容易提升產品品質的創新。

Answer 2

Teams create an environment of support and propel people toward implementation. A team environment can boost the confidence of individuals, allowing them to do their best work.

團隊能創造一個支持性的環境，並推動人們完成目標。團隊的環境能激發個人的信心，讓他們做到最好。

Answer 3

Good teams make the most of individual talents. Where one member may be weak, another might be strong, and working together they provide the perfect resource for an organization. Teams can create better communication and respectful relationships among employees.

好的團隊能最大化利用一個人的才能。當一個成員實力較弱，另一個實力較強時，他們一起合作就會為組織提供完美的資源。團隊可以使成員間產生更好地交流和互相尊重的關係。

Answer 4

For every advantage of working in a team, as there is the flip side. Just as "two heads are better than one," as we've all heard, "too many chefs spoil the broth." Basically, there are just too many people, too many ideas, and too many "experts" to come to an agreement and achieve a good result. It is simply why we have to constantly be reminded that there is no "I" in team.

每項團隊合作的優點背後，總會有缺點。正如「三個臭皮匠勝過一個諸葛亮」的反面即是「廚子多，做壞湯。」團隊中有太多的人、太多的想法、以及太多的「專家」，所以很難取得一個好的結果。這就是為什麼我們經常被提醒，團隊中沒有個人。

Answer 5

When people can't leave their egos behind, conflict and resentment arises. People become unwilling to open their minds to other perspectives and are intent on either forcing their point of view or not cooperating with others. The more conflict, the less innovation, and the farther the team gets from implementation and meeting goals.

當人們無法放下自尊時，就會引起爭端和怨恨。人們就會變得不願意開放心胸，從其他角度看待問題，他們要不就將自己的想法強加於他人，要不就是不願與他人合作。爭端愈多、創新愈少、團隊就離執行與目標愈遠。

Chapter 2

Answer 6

While a team has the potential to boost the individual members, if it is not functioning properly it can make some members feel inferior and unimportant. They contribute less and are discouraged from accessing their strong qualities. How much each person is contributing becomes the focus of the individuals. Relationships and communication worsens. The team is unsuccessful, and the individuals walk away worse off than when they started.

雖然團隊能激發人的潛力，但如果運轉不恰當，就會使一些成員覺得自己低人一等、不夠重要。他們為團隊做的貢獻較少，也不被鼓勵運用自己的長處。一個人為團隊做出多少貢獻，變成了個人的關注點。關係和溝通惡化，團隊合作不成功，個人離開時比他們加入團隊時的狀態還要糟糕。

≫ Q14　What experience do you have?
你有什麼樣的經驗？ track 022

當被問到這類的問題時，最重要的是詳細地表現自己的能力和經驗。注意將工作中獲得的經驗與當下你要應徵的職位做連結，以顯示你所擁有的經驗對眼前的工作是十分有幫助的，而你就是他們所需要的人才。同時注意回答時要秉持著誠實、勿誇大的態度。

Answer 1

I spent three years in sales at my previous company. Back then, I focused on growing customer base in the south and increased sales by 50% over a three-year period.

我在以前的公司做了三年銷售。那時候我專注於增加南部地區的客戶量，並在那三年時間，將銷售額提高了50%。

Answer 2

I worked hard to develop my computer skills in my last job, and this helped me to process customer management data more efficiently. I asked the company to send me on a training program to master the software, and it really paid off.

上一份工作時，我很努力提高我的電腦技能，這也幫助我更有效地處理客戶管理資料。我請求公司送我去上培訓課程，這非常值得。

Answer 3

In my previous position, I worked as part of a team on a number of projects. A big project I was involved with at my previous company was writing a new safety policy. It was a really in-depth project, so I put together a safety review committee. We worked together for a month to identify the safety needs of the various departments and what procedures would meet those needs. Our policy has been well accepted, and safety problems have decreased in all areas.

上一份工作時，我作為團隊成員，接手過很多案子。其中有個大型專案是編寫新的安全政策。這是一個很有深度的專案，所以我組織了一個安全複審協會。我們一起工作了一個月，確定各個部門的安全需要，以及符合這些需要的程序。我們的政策受到接受，所有領域的安全問題都減少了。

Answer 4

I pride myself on my customer service skills, and my ability to resolve what could be difficult situations. I have exceeded my sales goals every quarter and I've earned a bonus each year since I started with my current employer. My time management skills are excellent, and I'm organized, efficient, and take pride in excelling at my work.

我以自己的客戶服務技巧和解決複雜情況的能力為傲。從開始為我現在的雇主工作後，我每季的銷售額都會超過目標，並且每年都得到獎金。我的時間管理能力很棒，我有組織、有效率，並以我在工作中的優秀表現而驕傲。

>> **Q15　How do you handle pressure and stress?**
你怎樣處理工作壓力？ track 023

　　工作往往會給人帶來壓力，尤其是銀行、零售業等服務行業的工作。因此，面試官通常想要了解應徵者面對工作壓力的能力。在遇到這樣的問題時，你的回答所要表達的核心內容應是，你的抗壓能力很強，回答時可以舉一些過去對抗工作壓力的成功例子。

Answer 1

Stress is very important to me. With stress, I do the best possible job. The appropriate way to deal with stress is to make sure I have the correct balance between good stress and bad stress. I need good stress to stay motivated and productive.

壓力對我來說很重要。有了壓力，我能把工作做到最好。處理壓力

的最好方式就是確保我能在有利壓力和不良壓力之間平衡。我需要有利的壓力以保持積極性和高效率。

Answer 2

I find that when I'm under the pressure of a deadline, I can do some of my most creative work. I've done some of my best work under tight deadlines, where the atmosphere was very stressful.

我發現當處於臨近截止期的壓力下時，我能做出一些很有創造力的作品。我有一些精湛的作品就是在逼近截止日期、工作氛圍壓力很大的情況下完成的。

Answer 3

I'm not a person who has a difficult time with stress. When I'm under pressure, I focus and get the job done. I'm the kind of person who stays calm under pressure, and handles stress fairly easily.

我並不是一個不能承受壓力的人。當有壓力時，我集中精力完成工作。我是那種在壓力下能保持冷靜、輕易掌控壓力的人。

Answer 4

I plan and react to situations, not to pressure and stress. The best way to handle problems is to deflate them as quickly as possible with calm, diligent work—one step at a time. That way, the situation is handled and doesn't become stressful.

我就狀況做出計畫和反應，而不是針對壓力。處理問題的最好方式

就是通過冷靜勤奮的工作來釋放壓力———一步一步來。這樣一切狀況盡在掌握中，也就不會有壓力了。

Answer 5

Pressure and stress are part of the working world. I thrive under pressure. I bend and work harder, but I don't break. I find it exhilarating to be in a dynamic, challenging environment where the pressure is on.

壓力是工作的一部分。我從壓力中取得成功。我順應壓力、更加努力工作，但是我不會就此崩潰。我覺得處在一個有壓力、有活力具有挑戰性的環境中工作令人振奮。

Answer 6

From a personal perspective, I manage stress by visiting the gym every evening. It's a great stress reducer.

就個人角度來講，我透過每晚健身來釋放壓力。健身是個減少壓力好方式。

▶▶ Q16 What was the most and least rewarding about your job?
工作中最有收益和最沒有收益的是什麼？ track 024

　　這個問題在回答時必須注意不要將對眼前工作十分重要的部分說成是最沒有收益的。如果你認為某個部分最不能帶來收益，卻又是你眼下正應徵的工作中重要職責，這將會使你陷入十分尷尬的窘境。因此，以眼前工作的責任為中心，對於其中包含並占主導地位的職責，儘量將其美化，而你所討論最沒有收益的部分最好是與眼下應徵的工作無關緊要的內容。

Answer 1

The most rewarding part was that the skills and technology I learned will follow me wherever I go. However, I am a relational person, and the job didn't deal with that many people. Also, doing the same job every week can be boring.

最大的收益是我所學到的技術和技巧會伴隨我一生。但是我是個喜歡與人打交道的人，而之前的工作並不太需要與人打交道。而且每周重複同樣的工作很無聊。

Answer 2

I worked as an engineer in the commercial construction industry. The most rewarding part was seeing my hard work come to life in a way that affected the people who occupy the offices and schools that I helped design. The least rewarding aspect of my last job was my supervisor's failures in acknowledging great work.

我是一名商業建築行業的工程師。最大的收益就是能看見我的作品可以影響到在辦公室工作或在學校學習的人。最沒有收益的點是我的前上司無法發掘認同優秀的作品。

Answer 3

I enjoyed helping the clients identify their business challenges as well as assisting them in designing and implementing solutions. However, being abused by fussy customers was one of the least rewarding aspects.

我喜歡協助客戶確認他們的商業挑戰，並且幫助他們設計和實現解決方案。但是，有時會被吹毛求疵的客戶辱罵是最沒有收益的點。

Answer 4

The most rewarding part of my last job was that it allowed me to really expand my experience and knowledge, by seeing all sides of projects. My managers would make sure that each person would rotate technologies between projects. However, I didn't think the payment was appropriate.

上一份工作最大的收益是藉由認識專案的各個面向擴大了我的經驗和知識。經理會確保我們每個人輪流負責專案的不同技術層面，但是我覺得薪水並不合理。

NOTES

date: / /

📁 Q&A Time—About the Future 關於未來

》》Q1　What is the thing that most interests you about this job?
這份工作為什麼吸引你？ track 025

　　回答這個問題時，要切中要點，不要顯得太野心勃勃。答案要具體，可以說說這份工作一些細節上吸引你的內容，回答要真實。另外，可以表現自己是這個工作的合適人選，所以對這份工作有興趣，可以利用這個問題來表現自己的能力。

Answer 1

One of the things that really interests me is the opportunity to work in a team environment. I've always wanted to work with hard-working, professional, experienced people. I love contributing to a team effort, bringing out the best in myself and my teammates to fulfill our work goals and achieve top results.

我最感興趣的地方之一是能在團隊中工作。我一直想和努力、專業又有經驗的人一起工作。我喜歡向團隊貢獻我的努力，自己做到最好也讓隊友做到最好，一起合作完成工作目標，達到最好的結果。

Answer 2

This is not only a fine opportunity, but this company is a place where my qualifications can make a difference. It has enough challenges to keep me on my toes. That's the kind of job I like to anticipate every morning.

這不僅是個好機會，並且公司也很適合我的才能發揮。公司有很多挑戰可以讓我參與。這份工作正是我每天早晨想要趕赴的。

Answer 3

I want this job because it seems tailored to my competencies, which include sales and marketing. As I said earlier, in a previous position I created an annual growth rate of 22 percent. Additionally, the team I would work with looks terrific.

我想要這份工作是因為，它很適合我的銷售和行銷能力。正如我剛剛所說的，在之前的職位時，我將公司的銷售額提高了22%。另外，整個團隊看起來也很棒。

Answer 4

This job is a good fit for what I've been interested in throughout my career. It offers a nice mix of short-term and long-term activities. My short-term achievements keep me cranked up, and the long-term accomplishments make me feel like a million bucks.

這份工作完全符合我職業的興趣。它提供了短期和長期活動的完美結合。短期成就讓我興奮，而長期成就讓我更棒。

》 Q2　Why do you want this job?
你為什麼應徵這份工作？ track 026

　　這個問題可以從你所應徵的職業著手。談談這個職業吸引你的地方，結合自己的興趣做一定的解釋。當然，更重要的是為什麼

Chapter 2

是「這個公司」的「這份工作」，也就是說要結合你應徵的單位做闡述，像是誇讚一下你所應徵的單位，「可以給我更好地發展空間」、「有很好的前景」等。同時，表明自己的能力可以勝任這樣的工作，具體技巧和範例如下。

Answer 1

I feel I should have direct hands-on experience in this position at this stage of my career. I believe that this entry-level job may enhance my professional experience.

我認為在我職涯的這個階段，我應該有一些這個職位上的實戰經驗。我相信這個初階職位能夠為我增加我專業的經驗。

Answer 2

This position challenges me to keep up with the cutting edge of technologies. I believe it will allow me to utilize my skills to acquire in-depth experience in my profession for the benefit of this organization.

這份工作對我來說很有挑戰性，能讓我跟上新技術的步伐。我相信這份工作能讓我施展我的技能，從而獲得大量專業的經驗，為公司帶來利益。

Answer 3

The job is tailored to my skills and previous experience. I believe that this job will help me assume another level of responsibility in my career.

我認為這份工作就是為我的技能和先前的經驗量身打造的。我相信

這份工作能讓我在職業生涯中承擔的責任更上層樓。

Answer 4

I want to be a part of a company on its way up, as this company has already launched several top products. Being part of a research and development team is a job experience I always love to have.

貴公司已經發布了幾款尖端產品，而我想在公司發展的過程中成為它的一員。我總是希望能夠成為研究和發展團隊的一員。

Answer 5

I see this company not only as a positive work environment, but also as a good opportunity to have my skills and qualifications make a difference. This job in such a stable company offers long-term career development, and this is what I am looking for.

我認為貴公司不僅有著積極的工作環境，而且能夠為我提供發展技能和資格的好機會。發展穩定的公司可以提供給我長期的職業發展，而這正是我所尋找的。

Answer 6

This company is known as a company that rewards employees who deliver good results. Its good reputation and successful strategies and values make everyone want to work for such a company.

我知道貴公司以獎勵有優秀工作成果的員工而著稱。良好的名譽、

成功的戰略和價值觀，這使得每個人都希望自己能夠為這樣的公司工作。

▶▶ Q3 How would you describe your ideal job and your ideal work environment?
你理想的工作／工作環境是怎樣的？ 🔘 track 027

　　這個問題看似不重要，卻能將應徵者和其他學歷或工作經驗相當的人區分開來。如果被問到關於理想的工作，你可以向面試官表明你希望有一份能夠讓你的工作能力進步，以及能夠激發創造力的穩定工作。

Answer 1

I would love to work in a job in which I can work both by myself and with others to achieve the end result. I am very self-motivated, so I am interested in working in an atmosphere where I can continuously learn new things and improve my skills.

我喜歡這樣的工作：我既能獨自工作，又能與大家一起合作達成結果。我喜歡激勵自己，所以我有興趣在一個我一直能學到新東西以及提高自我技能的地方工作。

Answer 2

I flourish in an environment that allows me to grow my position and gives me learning opportunities. I like work environments where trust and team-work are keys to success. I really enjoy working with teams and feel mutual trust and respect is a necessary component to any job.

能夠讓我發展職位、給我學習的機會的工作環境能夠讓我工作表現更好。我喜歡的工作環境，信任和團隊合作是成功的關鍵。我真的很喜歡與團隊一起工作，感受大家互相信任和尊重是任何工作的必要成分。

Answer 3

I enjoy a workplace that gives enough space and helps employees to grow. There should be healthy team-work, good communication, and mutual understanding between each team member. I want a workplace where there is respect for an individual's ideas and where management always appreciates good work, as well as knowledge.

我喜歡一個能夠提供足夠的空間而且幫助員工成長的工作環境。要有一個健康的團隊合作，成員之間要有良好的溝通和互相的理解。我想要一個能夠尊重個人意見，管理部門總是欣賞優秀的工作和知識的工作環境。

Answer 4

I look for a stable job with quality supervision—a positive work culture at a successful company that will encourage me to work at my best. I want a job where my skills are utilized to the maximum and I can grow within the organization.

我想要一份有著高品質管理的穩定工作——在一家成功的公司，有著積極的企業文化，能夠鼓勵我盡自己的全力。我想要一個能夠把我的能力發揮到最大，而且我能在組織中成長的工作。

Answer 5

I would prefer the company culture to be very team-oriented, one that empowers employees to create and take initiative, and focuses on delivering real, measurable results, while still maintaining a friendly and respectful work environment.

我會更喜歡有團隊合作精神的公司，能夠讓員工積極創造、具有主動性，並且注重實行、可量化的工作成果，同時也能保持友好、互重的工作環境。

Answer 6

My ideal job would be: open, entrepreneurial, stimulating, collaborative, inspiring, focused on fostering strengths. One which provides the opportunity to learn, progress and contribute to the organization.

我理想的工作是——開放的、企業的、激勵的、合作的、鼓舞人心的，並且能夠注重培養員工的能力。一個提供機會學習、進步以及為組織貢獻（的工作）。

>> **Q4 What are your salary expectations?**
你的預期工資是多少？ track 028

　　首先，在求職面試中與面試官「商量」薪資是一件很有風險的事情。一般如果想討論薪資問題，請在確定已獲得這個職位後再提問。如果面試官主動問起這個問題，可以用一些技巧來回答。首先要做足準備工作，也就是對自己的價值評估和對這個公司薪資水準的了解，這樣才能做出比較適當的回應。當然，你也可以用一些其

他的技巧來躲過這個問題，像是「來這裡工作不是僅僅為了薪資，而是為了學習和發展的機會」等等。

Answer 1

I hope I can get around NT$32,000. Of course, the responsibility that goes along with this job is what interests me the most.

我希望我能拿到新臺幣32,000元左右的薪水。當然這份工作才是最吸引我的。

Answer 2

I hope I can get around NT$32,000. It also depends on my detailed responsibility.

我希望能有新臺幣32,000元左右的薪水。但這也要依我的工作能力來定。

Answer 3

My current salary is NT$32,000. I hope to get at least a 15% increase in my new job.

我目前的薪水是新臺幣32,000元。我希望這份新工作至少有15%的成長。

Answer 4

My salary expectations are open, based on the position, responsibilities, and total compensation package.

我的薪水期望依照職位、責任和整個薪資組合來定。

Answer 5

You want me to give you a salary I want for the position, but I am not sure what your position involves yet. I'm sorry, but I need more information about what kind of work you are expecting me to do for you.

您希望我提出希望待遇，但是我還不了解這個職位。很抱歉，但我需要更多資訊，了解您希望我做什麼類型的工作。

Answer 6

We can talk about salary once I have had a chance to review more details about the job and the benefit package available from your company. It does not make sense for me to talk about salary before knowing if I am a fit for the position. I am sure you are willing to offer a fair wage for the position.

我們可以再更深入了解這份工作，以及貴公司的福利待遇後討論薪資問題。在不知道我是否適合這個職位前就討論薪水問題沒有意義。我相信您會提供很公平的薪資。

Answer 7

I would like to table the issue of salary for the moment, until I know more about the job you will be asking me to do.

我希望暫且擱置這個問題，直到我更了解您將要求我做的這份工作。

Answer 8

I expect when we discuss salary, it will be within the range of salaries for this type of position in the industry. But that's really all I want to say about it right now.

我希望當我們討論薪資時，它與這個產業的這個職位情況相符。這是我目前唯一想說的。

Q5　What motivates you at work?
你工作的動力是什麼？ track 029

　　面試官提出這個問題是為了看應徵者是否有長遠的工作目標。在回答這個問題時，最好表示將職位和工作或是進步和學習的機會等當作自己的動力，而非薪資，這樣才能吸引面試官，讓對方認為你是為了工作而工作，而不是單為了薪資，也更能夠讓對方認為你就是他們需要的人才。

Answer 1

I am motivated by constant progress. I find it exciting to implement new ideas and see them through to fruition. I find the most satisfaction in implementing "out-of the-box" ideas that ultimately prove their value. I like to be challenged on the job and desire the opportunity to utilize my skills and talents. Quality leadership and culture in the workplace have allowed me to work at my best.

我工作的動力來自於不斷的進步。我覺得可以實現新想法、並取得成就令人很興奮。我覺得最令人滿足的是，可以實現「異想天開」的想法，而這些想法最終會證明它們自己的價值。我想要挑戰這份工作，渴望能有機會施展我的技能和才能。這裡的高品質領導和企業文化能夠讓我發揮最好的才能。

Answer 2

My motivator is working with what I've learned from key job assignments and experiences. I believe in making choices, tying them to circumstances, and taking corrective actions when necessary. I always want to try new things and ask for feedback that leads to improved results. And if my trying turns out to be a success, that will motivate me more.

我工作的動力就是，把我在重要工作任務中學到的東西和經驗用在現在的工作上。我相信工作時要做出選擇，將它們套用於特定的情況，並在必要時採取修正措施。我總是希望能夠嘗試新事物，並收到回饋，能使得結果更好。如果我的努力最終成功了，這就更能夠給我動力。

Answer 3

I was responsible for several projects where I directed development teams and implemented repeatable processes. The teams achieved 100% on-time delivery of software products. I am motivated both by the challenge of finishing projects ahead of schedule and by managing teams that achieve goals.

我曾經負責過幾個專案，工作是指揮發展團隊以及實施常規程序。這些團隊都達成準時遞交軟體產品。我的動力來自於提前完成專案的挑戰，以及管理團隊完成任務。

Answer 4

I've always been motivated by the desire to do a good job at whatever position I'm in. I want to excel and to be successful in my job, both for my own personal satisfaction and for my employer.

我的動力總是來自於無論在任何職位都要盡力做到最好。我希望在工作上勝出、成功，這既是為了讓我自己滿意也是為了讓老闆滿意。

Answer 5

I have always wanted to ensure that my company's clients get the best customer service I can provide. I've always felt that it's important, to me personally and for the company and clients, to provide a positive customer experience.

我總是要想確保公司客戶得到我能提供的最好客戶服務。我一直認為提供正面的客戶體驗很重要，對我和對公司和客戶來說都是。

Answer 6

I love working with people on a day-to-day basis. Interacting with people is what gets me out of bed every morning. I love the excitement of making a sale and having a new customer on my list.

我喜歡每天和人一起工作。和人打交道是我每天上班的動力。我喜歡做銷售，每增添一名新客戶我都很高興。

Chapter 2

▶▶ Q6　Are you willing to travel or relocate?
你願意出差或外派嗎？　 track 030

　　這個問題照實回答就好，如果你由於家庭原因不願意外派或經常出差，用人單位也會理解。如果你是這樣的情況，一般可以說，偶爾的出差可以接受，但由於家庭原因，不希望太頻繁地出差或長期外派。

Answer 1

It's my pleasure. Because if you want me to relocate or travel, it means you think of me as a leading person. By these, I will learn more things and gain more knowledge about the company. The most important thing is that it will add one more experience to my life.

這是我的榮幸。因為如果您希望我外派或者出差，這表示您認為我是個領導角色的人。通過出差和外派，我可以學到更多東西，並更了解公司。最重要的是，這也會為我的人生經歷添上新的一筆。

Answer 2

Location doesn't matter to me. I can give my best performance anywhere because I love my job and my responsibilities, and I want to get some experience from any kind of environment. Experience makes a man perfect.

地點對我來說不是問題。不管在哪我都能很好發揮我的能力，因為我愛我的工作和職責，並且我也希望從各種環境中吸取經驗。經驗使人完美。

Answer 3

Depending upon the demands of the organization, if I need to relocate or travel, then I will do it without any hesitation. It would be my pleasure to go because I could get knowledge and experience in different locations.

根據公司的需要，如果我必需外派或出差，我會毫不猶豫接受。這是我的榮幸，因為我能在不同的地方學到更多知識、累積更多經驗。

Answer 4

In an organization, relocation is a common thing. If you give me the opportunity to relocate my job, then I will be very happy to relocate to some other place. It will give me greater experience and enhance my knowledge.

在組織中外派是很常見的。如果公司給我機會外派，我會很樂意外派到別的地方。這能豐富我的經驗，並擴大我的見識。

Answer 5

I don't have any problem with relocating or traveling to other places. It's not a big matter because I can adapt myself to any environment. I'm always interested in going to new places and meeting new people.

外派或是出差對我來說都沒有問題。這沒什麼大不了，因為我能適應各種環境。我對去新的地方、認識新的人總是很感興趣。

Chapter 2

Answer 6

I can relocate or travel to any place, and it is my strength to change myself according to the environment. It is nothing new for me to relocate or travel to new places because I've already relocated three times.

我可以外派或出差到任何地方，根據環境改變自己是我的強項。外派或是出差對我來說已經不新鮮了，因為我已經外派三次了。

⟫ Q7 Are you willing to work overtime?
你願意加班嗎？ track 031

面試時，無論遇到什麼問題，回答都應誠實，面對這個問題時，當然也不例外。除非你真的很願意加班，否則答案不要只是簡單的「願意」兩個字。首先，你可以表明以自己的能力與效率，能夠在工作時間內完成自己的任務，不會將工作拖到需要加班的程度。其次，你可以表示如果確實需要加班，偶爾的加班是沒有問題的。

Answer 1

It depends on the work I have to do and my ability to perform it. If I have the capability to complete it, I don't mind working overtime. However, if I didn't have the ability to complete the task, it would be risky to take it over.

這要看我需要做的工作和我的工作能力了。如果我有能力完成一項工作，我不介意加班。但如果我沒有足夠的能力來完成這任務，接下這份工作恐怕只是有風險。

Answer 2

I won't mind working overnight for a couple of days or even weeks in times of tight deadlines. However, I hope the projects are scheduled properly so that working overtime is not too common.

如果時間緊迫的話，我不介意加幾天，甚至是幾周的班。但是我希望工作專案都能有適當的計畫，這樣加班就不會變成家常便飯。

Answer 3

I am a very responsible person. I have definite planning, and I go with that in a systematic way, so in case I am behind schedule, I will surely work overnight and make sure I complete it in time.

我是一個很有責任心的人。我有一定的計畫，並且能夠系統性地按照計畫來做事，因此如果我進度比計畫慢，我一定會連夜趕工，保證按時完成任務。

Answer 4

I do understand that it will occasionally be necessary in the software industry to work overtime. Generally, I feel that the work can be completed on time if we work hard and utilize the work hours well. However, I have no problem working overtime if the project deadlines are very tight and require me to do so.

我明白在軟體產業有時必須加班。一般來說，我覺得如果我們認真

Chapter 2

工作、合理利用工作時間，任務是可以按時完成的。但是如果專案的截止日期很緊，需要加班，我是完全沒有問題的。

》Q8 Why should we hire you?
我們為什麼要聘用你？ track 032

　　這又是一個展示自我的機會，但是與自我介紹和談談自己的優點這兩個問題有所不同，這個問題在回答時，要更注重將自身的優點和公司結合起來。也就是要強調自己能為公司做出哪些貢獻，這才是面試官所想聽到的內容。

Answer 1

As a freshman in the workplace, I can adapt myself to any type of environment. I will put all my efforts towards your company's success. I will apply innovative ideas, work hard, and learn new things eagerly for the development of your company in such a competitive industry.

作為一名職場新人，我能適應任何環境。我會為了公司的成功全心努力。我會運用創新的想法、認真地工作、積極地學習新事物，為公司在如此競爭的產業中謀發展。

Answer 2

As I am a freshman, I can't say that I am the best for our organization, but I think you can hire me because I can easily mingle with team members and will give my best for the company's development. If you give me this wonderful opportunity, then I will definitely do my best to give a good effort, with punctuality and honesty.

因為我是個新人，我不敢說我是公司的最佳人選，但是你們絕對可以聘用我，因為我可以很容易就融入團隊中，並且為了公司發展拚盡全力。如果您能給我這難得的機會，我絕對會按時地、誠實地做到最好。

Answer 3

The dedication and honesty in me separates me from other guys. I have the right combination of skills and experience for this job. I also bring the additional qualities of strong analytical and problem-solving abilities, as shown in my introduction at my previous company.

我的奉獻精神和誠實品格讓我脫穎而出。我有適合這份工作的技術和經驗結合。如同我在自我介紹時提過的，我在前公司還磨練了額外強大的分析和解決問題的能力。

Answer 4

You should hire me not just because I am highly qualified. You should hire me because I know what I do. Many people don't realize what and why they are doing something. For work, we need to know what we are doing, and then the work experience will come. And when we realize what our job is, we will do our best because of our interest.

您應該僱用我不僅是因為我的能力很高。您應該僱用是因為我知道自己在做什麼。很多人不明白他們在做什麼，或為何而做。工作上，我們必須知道自己在做什麼，才能得到相應的工作經驗。當我

們意識到我們的工作，我們就會因為興趣而做到最好。

Q9 What do you expect from your supervisor?
你對主管有哪些預期？ track 033

面試官問這個問題的時候，主要是想看應徵者對於你未來的主管是否有合理的預期，並看應徵者是否會利用這個問題來評價前主管。如果你談論一些你前主管不好的地方，那小心，你就會黑掉了。面試的一條鐵規則是——千萬不要在面試官面前抱怨你之前的上司，這會給面試官留下很不好的印象。因此，正確的回答方式是儘量將答案集中在你認為主管應該擁有的優良特質上，而不是抱怨。

Answer 1

I appreciate a work environment where supervisors try to make personal connections with their employees. In my last job, I liked the fact that management did not show favoritism, and they understood employees' needs, as well as their strengths. Of course, these things take time to learn, but I would want my supervisor to try to know me in that way.

我喜歡的工作環境是主管努力和員工建立人際關係。在我上一份工作中，我很欣賞上司能夠不偏不倚，他們了解員工的需要以及長處。當然，這些情況需要時間才能得知，但我希望我的上司能夠試著用這種方式認識我。

Answer 2

I would like to be able to go to my manager if I had an issue or idea. I would like to be able to feel comfortable to express my thoughts. I would also expect my supervisor to be open and honest with me, and to let me know if there was anything I could do to improve or change in my work.

如果我有問題或是想法，我希望能夠與我的上司交流。我希望能夠自在地表達自己的想法。我也希望我的上司能夠對我開放而誠懇，如果在工作上有任何我能改善或是改變的事都讓我知道。

Answer 3

I would like my supervisor to have the proper qualities to guide his or her employees. He should have a decision-taking tendency and be able to control his team and team members. He must have the capacity to lead the team according to circumstances.

我希望我的上司有適當的能力指引下屬。他必須能傾向於做決定，並能掌控他的團隊和成員。他必須要有根據環境變化領導團隊的能力。

Answer 4

I would like my supervisor to have honest and open communication with me. He could recognize me for my efforts and the value I provide to the company, and treat me with respect and equality.

我希望我的上司和我能有坦誠、開放的交流。他能認同我為公司所做的貢獻和價值，尊重我並公平地對待我。

>> **Q10** **Have you ever had difficulty with your boss? If the boss is wrong, how do you handle it?**
你和上司有過不愉快的經歷嗎？如果上司犯錯你會如何處理？ track 034

　　這兩個問題主要是用來看應徵者如何處理與上司之間的關係，和這方面的能力。一般來說，你可以選擇說你與上司之間沒有出現過問題或是不愉快的經驗，或者簡單描述一些小問題就好。回答時要表示對上司的尊敬，同時也要表示自己是個正直的人。當然還是那句老話，千萬不要在面試官面前抱怨你先前的上司。

Answer 1

I had a rocky start with a manager once, because we had different expectations for the flow of the workday. Once we talked about it, we realized that our goals were very compatible, and we were able to work very successfully together for several years. I have found that if I take the time to talk with my manager at the beginning of a project, we can all get off to a great start on the same page.

曾經我和經理有個不愉快的開端，因為我們對一天的工作流程期望不同。但當我們交談後，我們發現我們的目標是相符的，然後我們一起成功地合作了好幾年。我發現如果在專案開始的時候，我就和經理進行交談，我們就能有一個好的開端。

Answer 2

My last boss had less experience than most of the people

she managed. But she didn't mind hearing that she was doing something wrong, as long as the right way was explained. If I told her "It might work better if we try it this way," she'd say "OK, try it."

我的上一任老闆比她的所有雇員都資歷要淺。但是只要說明正確的方法，她並不介意聽到她做錯某事。如果我告訴她：「如果我們這樣做可能效果會更好」，她就會說：「好的，那就試試」。

Answer 3

It was an important project, and the boss was dead wrong about the hardware needed to run a new Internet service. I went into his office armed to the teeth with all the proof, and convinced him about what needed to be changed. He had me accompany him to report the new hardware needs to his boss. We spun it as a better solution, not that the original solution was wrong. It was a win-win for both of us and for the company.

在一個很重要的專案中，關於硬體需要安裝一個新的網路服務，我的上司犯了大錯。我帶著證據，全副武裝地走進他的辦公室，最終說服他某些地方需要改變。他讓我陪同他將這一新的硬體需求彙報給他的上司。我們告訴他的上司說這是一個更好的方案，而不是上一個方案有問題。這對我們和對公司來說是雙贏。

Answer 4

I would say that I have never really had a problem working with anyone. I try to find our common ground, and get along with everyone and every personality.

我可以說，我從沒和任何人在工作上有過什麼問題。我試著找出我們的共同點，與每個不同個性的人和睦相處。

>> Q11　Where do you want to be five years from now?
　　　Where do you see yourself in five years?
　　　你未來五年的計畫是什麼？ track 035

　　這個問題是招聘者用來考量應徵者是否對將來的工作有一定的規劃以及抱負。一般來說，回答要求較為具體，比如五年內的目標是某個職位等。另外，回答一定要表明自己努力的決心。

Answer 1

Five years down the line, I would like to see myself as an important part of the organization. Also, there would be a great value added to the organization by me. Lastly, I will be someone who will have the ability to make any fruitful decision.

我希望五年後自己能夠成為公司中重要的一分子。我也能夠為公司帶來附加的價值。最後，我能有能力決定任何有益的決策。

Answer 2

After five years, I would like to see myself as a senior executive of your organization, where I could use my full knowledge and experience to raise the company to the top.

我希望五年後，我能在公司擔任高級主管的職位，這樣我就可以全面發揮自己的知識和經驗，幫助公司達到頂尖的位置。

Answer 3

After five years, I would like to be in a position where I would be admired and recognized by everyone for my achievements at work.

我希望五年之後，我能夠在一個大家都尊敬的職位上，並且工作上的成就能夠得到大家的認可。

Answer 4

After five years, I can see myself as a top performing employee in a well-established organization, like this one. I plan on enhancing my skills and continuing my involvement in related professional associations.

五年後，我會是個像貴公司一樣信譽卓越的公司中表現傑出的雇員。我計畫提升我的技能，繼續保持相關專業的密切聯繫。

>> **Q12 How long would you like to stay with this company?**
你會在本公司服務多久呢？ track 036

　　面試官問這個問題往往是想看應徵者是否能夠長久地在此單位工作，穩定性夠不夠高。如果應徵者穩定性不夠，那麼就意味著公司不久之後就需要重新再招人，這對公司來說是件很麻煩的事，因為得重新面試、訓練。因此，在回答這個問題時，應徵者應表示自己能夠長久穩定地在本單位工作。

Answer 1

I would like to stay as long as there are growth opportunities.

Chapter 2

只要有成長的機會，我就會一直待在這裡。

Answer 2

I would prefer to stay long-term, if possible. I like the flexible hours you offer, which would work well with my other commitments, like my studies, children, and family.

如果可能的話，我會長期待在這裡。我很喜歡這裡彈性的工作時間，讓我能好好地處理其他的責任，像是學習、孩子和家庭。

Answer 3

I will stay as long as I can continue to learn and to grow in my field.

只要我能在我的領域繼續學習和長進，我就會留在這裡。

Answer 4

As long as I know I'm still very productive in the company, and you lay your trust on me, I will stay in the company.

只要我還能為公司效勞，並且你們信任我，我就會一直待在這裡。

≫ Q13 What can you do to ensure a successful team environment?
你會怎麼做來保證團隊合作的成功？ track 037

在求職面試中，面試官會考驗應徵者團隊合作的能力。常見的提問方式是「你會怎麼做來保證團隊合作的成功？」在回答這個問題時，注意按角色不同來給出不同的答案。通常，可以分別以經理的身分和以普通職員的身分來回答這個問題。

Answer 1

As manager of a team, I will set clear, specific expectations and have a dialogue with my employees to be certain they understand these expectations. It is important that they not only understand the goals, but also the reason the team has been created.

作為團隊經理，我會設定清楚、具體的目標，並且與成員對話，以保證他們理解目標。重要的是，不僅要讓成員們明白目標，也要讓他們明白團隊建立的原因。

Answer 2

I will understand my role in a team and own it. I will try to be a problem solver. I won't look to place blame and will not focus on the negative. And I will stand up and make things better, rather than sitting back and complaining.

我會弄清我在團隊的位置然後負責。我會試著成為一個能解決問題的人。我不會推卸責任、集中在負面思考。我會挺身而出、試著改善狀況，而不是躲在後面抱怨。

Answer 3

Being a team member, I want to be supported by the team, and I know this can only happen if I support others. I will take the time to listen to others in the group. I will open my mind and realize teamwork takes patience, understanding, and mutual respect and support.

作為一個團隊成員，我希望團隊能支援我，而且我也知道，只有我也支持別人，別人才會支持我。我會花時間傾聽團隊中其他人的想法。我也會敞開心胸，明白團隊合作需要耐心、理解和互相尊重及支持。

Answer 4

I will feel good about myself if I can help the team by making it better for everyone. A negative attitude can be contagious, and so can a positive one. I will constantly practice tolerance and keep communication open with all members of the team.
如果能為每個人幫助改善團隊，我會感覺很好。消極的想法會傳染，同理，積極的想法也會傳染。我會持續包容，並且保持團隊成員間的公開溝通。

NOTES

date: /   /

面試後的備忘錄

面試結束並不意味著應徵者的工作已結束，因為接下來還有一系列的事情需要應徵者去完成。以下是一些應聘者在面試後需要做的工作：

1. **Immediately send a follow-up letter.**
   立刻發一封後續信。

   無論應徵的職位種類，應徵者都應在面試後一天內發一封感謝信。感謝信不需要很長，但卻有一些需要注意的地方。

Example 1

Dear Mr./Ms.,

I want to thank you for taking the time to interview me yesterday for the position of [position name] . I sincerely enjoyed meeting with you and learning more about the [job name] and your company.

After our conversation, and while observing the company's operations, I am convinced that my [area of experience] experience fits me out more than adequately for the job, and my background and skills can take the company to new heights of success. I believe I can make a significant contribution to the [new project name] . I am excited by your interest in [idea you suggested] , and I also have a number of great ideas for [you have great ideas for...] . I feel

Chapter 2

confident that my experience in [your experience in...] would enable me to fill the job requirements effectively.

As you know (I neglected to mention during my interview that), my work as [previous position] at [previous working place] provided an excellent background, as well as an understanding of all the aspects of this kind of job. In addition to my enthusiasm, I will bring excellent qualifications, skills, assertiveness and the ability to [your ability] to this position. I am more convinced than ever that I will fit in beautifully as a member of the team and contribute my skills and talents for the benefit of your company.

Please feel free to contact me if I can provide you with any further information. I can make myself available for any further discussions of my qualifications that may be needed. I thank you again for considering me for this position. I am very interested in working for you, and am looking forward to hearing from you concerning your hiring decision.

Sincerely,

Eason Chen

先生 / 女士您好：

謝謝您昨天為我費時進行的（職位名稱）面試。我為能與您交

流感到衷心的高興，並且對貴公司和此職位有了更多的了解。

　　在與您交談及看過貴公司的運行之後，我確信我的（某領域）的經驗使我對這個職位來說再合適不過了，還有我的背景和技能也定能幫助貴公司上升到新的成功階段。我相信我能給（新專案的名稱）帶來顯著的貢獻。您對（某觀念）的興趣讓我大感興奮，同時我對（某方面）也有著許多的工作理念。我有自信我在（某方面）的經驗使得我很符合這個職位的要求。

　　您知道的（或是我在面試中忘了說），我之前於（某公司）的（某職位）的工作給予了我很好的背景，和對此類工作的全面理解。加上我的熱情，對於這份工作，我有優秀的條件、技能、魄力和（某方面的）能力。更讓我確定的是，我會完美地融入到貴公司的團隊中，並施展我的才能，為公司做出貢獻。

　　如果我能提供更多的資訊，請隨時聯繫我。我有時間與您深度討論這份工作，及任何需要的資格。再一次感謝您能夠考慮由我勝任這份工作。我很有興趣能夠為您工作，期待著您的聘請回應。

謹上

陳伊森

Example 2

Dear Mr./Ms.,

　　Thanks for taking the time to discuss the [position] and my experience in [area of experience] with me. I really enjoyed speaking with you yesterday.

After meeting with you, I am sure that my background and skills fit your needs. Your plans for [plans of your employer for] sound exciting, and I hope I can contribute to your future success. I think my background in [background in] makes me an asset to your company. I was impressed with your department's energy and positive attitude. I know I would enjoy working with you and your group.

I look forward to hearing from you concerning your hiring decision. If I may be of any assistance, feel free to email or call me again at [your phone number]. I appreciate your consideration.

Sincerely,

Eason Chen

先生 / 女士您好：

感謝您能費時與我討論關於（某職位）以及我於（某方面）的經驗。我真的很高興昨天能與您進行面談。

在與您面談之後，我確信我的背景和技能十分符合您的要求。您對於（你要應徵的職位）的計畫聽起來很棒，我希望我能為您將來的成功出一份力。我認為我在（某方面）的背景使得我對於貴公司是十分有價值的。貴部門的活力和積極的態度讓我印象深刻。我相信我一定能與您和您的團隊工作愉快。

期待著您的聘用回應。如果我能幫上忙，請隨時用email或撥打（你的電話號碼）聯繫我。感謝您的考慮。

謹上

陳伊森

2. Check in with your references.
聯繫你的推薦人。

所謂的推薦人就是在履歷表中，或面試時你所提及的過去工作夥伴或是上司，他們能夠給予面試官一些關於你的參考意見，也就是你在過去工作中的表現，或是你的工作能力或風格等等。然而，如果當面試官找到他們，問一些關於你的情況時，他們卻不記得你，或是說對你的印象不深，這是十分尷尬的情況。因此，在面試之後，和你的推薦人取得聯繫，幫助他們回憶一下你，或是給他們留下一些印象，也是必要的程序。注意態度不要太魯莽，或是把目的直接告訴你的推薦人。記住你的最終目的是給推薦人留下好印象，讓他們為你做出正面的推薦，進而給可能成為你未來老闆的人留下一個好印象。因此，在聯繫溝通的過程中，好的印象是最重要的。如果你的推薦人對你印象並不深刻，你可以提及一些過去工作中積極的事例來讓他回想起你的優秀特質。

3. Review your social media profiles.
檢閱你的社交媒體檔案。

在資訊化的今天，網路發達，你在網上發布的任何資訊都有可能被你所應徵的單位所看到。尤其是面試之後，如果他們對你感興趣，可能會查閱你在網上的社交媒體檔案，對你有更深入的了解。因此，

這時你的社交媒體檔案就顯得十分重要。面試之後，記得查閱你的社交媒體檔案，以顯得你更加適合你所應徵的職位。不要在社交媒體上顯示任何關於面試的負面情況，這對於你是百害無一利的。

4. Use your one phone call.
打一次電話。

面試後打一次電話詢問結果是可以的。在這裡需要強調的是，可以打一次電話，而並非需要打一次電話。一般而言，我們建議用電子郵件的方式進行後續的溝通，如前面所提到的用電子郵件的方式發感謝信等。然而，如果應徵者想打電話進行進一步的溝通，或是詢問面試結果，以一次為上限。太多的電話來訪只會讓用人單位感到厭煩，如果他們還未決定，那這些電話無疑增加了他們對應徵者的負面印象，對於應徵者的面試結果是相當不利的。因此，**只能打一次電話**是面試後需要注意的要點。

NOTES

date: / /

Chapter 3
面試實錄大透析

📁 行政秘書 Administrative Assistant track 038

》Q1 **What computer skills do you have, and what programs are you comfortable using?**
你有哪些電腦技能？你擅長使用哪些程式？

Answer 1-1

I'm proficient with Microsoft Word, Excel, Access, and Power Point. I'm very comfortable using these programs and have a lot of experience doing so. I'm interested in learning how to use other programs as well.
我精通微軟的Word、Excel、資料庫管理系統和 Power Point。我擅長使用這些軟體並有豐富 的使用經驗。同時我也對學習其他的電腦程式 很感興趣。

Answer 1-2

I'm very comfortable using computers, and I am confident in my ability to learn any new programs quickly.
我很擅長使用電腦，並且能夠快速學習使用新的 程式。

Chapter 3

▶▶**Q2** **Are you comfortable using a phone with multiple lines and handling a high volume of telephone calls?**
你能使用多線電話以及應付大量的通話嗎？

Answer 2-1

Yes, I'm comfortable using multiple phone lines with a high volume of calls, and have done so in the past. I'm able to keep the conversations separated, and deal with the clients in a friendly, efficient manner.

可以，我擅長應付大量的多線電話，曾經有過這樣的經驗。我能夠分別保持不同的通話，並能友善、有效率地與客戶交流。

Answer 2-2

I haven't directly handled multiple phone lines, but I understand the importance of being courteous and efficient, and I'm a quick learner.

我還沒有直接進行過多線通話，但我了解禮貌和效率的重要性，而且我學習新事物很快。

Answer 2-3

I understand that phone contact is often the first interaction that a customer has with the company, and the first impression is extremely important. It is critical to maintain a friendly, professional manner on the phone at all times.

我知道電話溝通往往是顧客與公司第一次互動，而第一印象非常重要。通話時持續保持友好和專業態度非常重要。

»Q3 **At this company, we like to think of ourselves as a team that works together toward the same goals. How do you feel about working in a team environment?**
我們希望將自己看作一個團隊，並向著同樣的目標努力。你如何看待在團隊中工作？

Answer 3-1

I enjoy working in a team environment, and I get along well with people. In my past work experience, I implemented a system to help organize the communication between my co-workers to enhance our productivity as a team.

我很喜歡在團隊中工作，並且我擅長與人相處。在我過去的工作經驗中，我曾運用一個系統來幫助組織同事間的溝通，並提高整體團隊的生產力。

Answer 3-2

I believe that I have a lot to contribute to a team environment, and I am comfortable in both leadership and player roles. I'm outgoing, friendly, and have strong communication skills.

我相信我能為團隊環境做出很多貢獻，而且作為領導者或成員對我都不是問題。我很外向、為人友善並且有很強的溝通技巧。

▶▶ Q4 How would you feel supervising two or three other employees?
你覺得管理兩三個員工怎麼樣？

Answer 4-1

I would be comfortable in a leadership position. I have had the opportunity to supervise several employees in the past, and was able to utilize each individual's talents as a part of our team.

我很擅長領導工作。我過去曾有機會管理過幾個員工，並且利用團隊中每個人的才能。

Answer 4-2

In a leadership position, I feel that it's important to encourage an environment where teamwork is emphasized, and each individual feels that they are making a real contribution to the best of their abilities.

在領導的位置上，我認為要鼓勵強調團隊精神的環境，並要讓每個人都感到他們真正為這個團隊貢獻自己最好的能力。

▶▶ Q5 Give some examples of teamwork.
舉一些團隊合作的例子。

Answer 5-1

In my last position, I was part of a software implementation team. We all worked together to plan and manage the implementation schedule, to provide customers with training, and to ensure a smooth transition for our customers. Our team always completed our projects ahead of schedule with very positive reviews from our clients.

在上一個工作職位中，我是軟體安裝組的成員。我們一起合作計畫和管理安裝進度、提供客戶培訓、確保客戶順利地轉換。我們團隊總是提前完成專案，並且得到客戶的好評。

Answer 5-2

I was part of a team responsible for evaluating and selecting a new vendor for our office equipment and supplies. The inter-departmental team reviewed options, compared pricing and service, chose a vendor, and implemented the transition to the new vendor.

我曾經待過一個團隊，是負責評估和選擇新的辦公設備與補給品項供應商。這個跨部門的團隊評估各種選擇、比對不同的價格及服務、選擇供應商、並完成轉換到新廠商的工作。

Answer 5-3

In high school, I enjoyed playing soccer and performing with the marching band. Each required a different kind of team play, but the overall goal of learning to be a member of a group was invaluable. I continued to grow as a team member while on my sorority's debate team and through my advanced marketing class, where we had numerous team assignments.

高中時，我喜歡踢足球，並在軍樂隊中演出。這兩者需要不同的團

隊合作，但學習當個團隊成員的整體目標是非常珍貴的。我因持續作為團隊成員而成長，在大學姐妹會的辯論隊，以及透過高階行銷課中，有很多的團隊任務。

》》Q6　How do you handle stress and pressure?
你怎樣應對壓力？

Answer 6-1

I find that when I'm under the pressure of a deadline, I can do some of my most creative work.

我發現當我迫於截止期限的壓力時，最能發揮我的創造力。

Answer 6-2

I find it exhilarating to be in a dynamic environment where the pressure is on.

我覺得在一個有壓力的、活躍的環境中工作令人十分振奮。

Answer 6-3

I'm not a person who has a difficult time with stress. When I'm under pressure, I focus and get the job done.

我對壓力處理沒有問題。當我有壓力時，我會集中精力、並完成工作。

》Q7　What is your greatest strength, and how will it help your performance in this position?
你最大的強項是什麼？它如何能夠幫助你在這份工作的表現？

Answer 7-1

My organizational skill is one of my greatest strengths. In my previous administrative assistant position, I restructured the office filing system to make it easier to access client charts and information quickly and efficiently. This experience will enhance my performance in this position because I'm able to keep things organized and neat, which means I get more tasks completed in a shorter amount of time.

我最大的強項之一是組織能力。在我之前的行政助理工作中，我重整了公司的檔案管理系統，使其能夠更容易、快速有效地找出客戶的圖表與資料。這一經驗能提升我在這份工作上的表現，因為我可以將檔案整理得有序而整潔，也就是說我能在更短的時間裡能完成更多的任務。

Answer 7-2

My ability to work with many different people. I enjoy learning from everyone I meet, and in this position I believe that will enhance my ability to perform on the team.

我最大的強項是與不同的人一起工作。我很喜歡從遇到的每個人身上學習，而在這個職位上，我相信這能提升我團隊工作表現的能力。

Answer 7-3

My greatest strength is my ability to focus on my work. I'm not easily distracted, and this means that my performance is very high, even in a busy office like this one.

我最大的強項是能夠專注於我的工作。我不容易分心，尤其是在這樣一個忙碌的公司裡，我的工作效率很高。

》》單字片語練功坊

1. proficient *adj.* 精通的；熟練的
2. be comfortable + V-ing 做...很順手
3. efficient *adj.* 有效率的
4. handle *vt.* 處理
5. interaction *n. [U]* 互動
6. impression *n. [C]* 印象
7. professional *adj.* 專業的
8. implement *vt.* 實施；執行
9. enhance *vt.* 提高；增加
10. productivity *n. [U]* 生產力
11. contribute to *vi.* 貢獻
12. supervise *vt.* 監督；管理
13. utilize *vt.* 使用；運用
14. ensure *vt.* 確保；保證
15. pressure *n. [U]* 壓力
16. access *vt.* 使用；取用

電話客服 Call Center track 039

》Q1 Are you able to maintain accuracy while handling a large number of calls?
你在處理大量的通話時，能保持正確性嗎？

Answer 1-1

I am able to handle a large number of calls without my accuracy being compromised.
我能在處理大量的通話時，不讓我的正確性受到影響。

Answer 1-2

My accuracy has never been affected by the number of calls I am handling.
我的正確性從不受通話數量的影響。

Answer 1-3

My accuracy during the last 5 years has always been over 95%.
在過去的五年中，我的正確性在95%以上。

Chapter 3

>> **Q2** **Describe how you would handle a problem you were having with a co-worker.**
談談你是怎麼處理與同事間的問題。

Answer 2-1

If I were having a problem with a co-worker, I would try talking to them to see if we could work out our differences. If they weren't open to that, or if the problem remained, I would discuss it with my supervisor.

如果我與同事間存在問題，我會試著與他們進行交談，看看能不能解決異見。如果他們不夠放開心胸，或問題一直存在，我會與我的上司討論。

Answer 2-2

I would first talk to the person and try to figure out what was bothering him. If the problem continued after talking to him, I would bring it to the attention of my supervisor. In my experience, what can't be resolved by talking one on one with the co-worker should be brought to the supervisor right away, before it escalates.

首先，我會和他談談，試著找到他的困擾處。如果談過之後問題還存在，我就會把問題讓我的上司注意到。以我的經驗，如果在與同事談過後還存在的問題，在其加劇之前，應該要立刻讓上司知道。

Answer 2-3

I try to get along with everyone, and respect their opinions and boundaries. In the past, when I have had a problem with someone, I have been able to work it out by talking with them.

我努力和大家和平相處，尊重他們的意見和底線。以前當我和某人之間出現問題的話，我總能經過交談來解決。

》》Q3 Do you have experience handling multiple phone lines?
你能應對多線通話嗎？

Answer 3-1

This is the first call center position I have applied for, but in the training I have done through the temp agency I have been working with, I practiced with multiple lines, and was able to handle them with ease.

這是我應徵的第一個電話客服職位，但我之前曾與臨時就業服務站工作與訓練，我練習過多線電話，並且應對得很輕鬆。

Answer 3-2

I have over 10 years of experience working with multiple phone lines, in a busy doctor's office, as well as at the call center where I worked previously.

我有超過十年的經驗應對多線電話，在忙碌的醫生辦公室工作過，也在之前的電話客服中心工作過。

Answer 3-3

Yes, I do. In my last position, I had multiple lines coming to me, which I had no difficulty handling.

是的，我可以。在我上一個職務中，我有過接聽多線電話的經驗，我處理起來毫不費力。

Q4 Do you have good people skills?
你與人相處的能力好嗎？

Answer 4-1

I like working with people, and I have been told that I have good people skills. I think I communicate effectively and in a pleasant way.

我喜歡和大家一起工作，大家也都說我與人相處的能力不錯。我覺得我能有效並愉快地與人溝通。

Answer 4-2

I get along well with most people I meet, and people find me easy to talk to, so I think I have good people skills.

我與遇到的大多數人相處得都很好，大家覺得與我交談起來很容易，所以我認為我與人相處的能力很強。

Answer 4-3

Throughout my career, I have always worked in customer service, and been known as a people person.

在我的職涯中，我一直從事客戶服務工作，大家都知道我是個與人相處的高手。

Chapter 3

Q5 How are your talk and type skills?
你的口語能力和打字能力如何？

Answer 5-1

Excellent. My typing speed and accuracy stay very high while I am making calls.

非常好。我通話時的打字速度和準確率都很高。

Answer 5-2

Talking and typing come naturally to me. I have always been good at multi-tasking.

我很善於講話和打字，我一直很擅長多工任務。

Answer 5-3

My talk and type skills are very good, and are constantly improving.

我講話和打字的能力都很好，並且還不斷提升中。

≫ Q6 Have you ever had difficulty getting along with a manager?
你與上司間曾出現過問題嗎？

Answer 6-1

Once I had a manager who brought her own problems into work with her on a daily basis. She was going through a difficult time in her personal life, which everyone tried to sympathize with, but it affected the atmosphere at work in a negative way. This made her very difficult to get along with.

以前我有一個上司每天都把自己的問題帶到工作中。當時她個人正經歷一段困難的時期，大家都很同情，但它對於工作氣氛帶來了負面影響。這讓她變得很難相處。

Answer 6-2

No, I am a hard worker, and my managers always seem to appreciate the job I'm doing. I've gotten along well with every manager I've had.

沒有過，我工作很努力，我的上司都很欣賞我的工作。我與每一位上司相處的都很好。

》》 **Q7 Do you multi-task well, or do you prefer to tackle one problem at a time?**
你能同時進行多項任務嗎？還是說你更喜歡一次解決一個問題？

Answer 7-1

I am fantastic at multi-tasking, in my personal as well as my professional life. I prefer having many things going on at once to completing one thing before moving to another.

我同時進行多項任務的能力很棒，無論是個人生活上還是工作上。比起做完一件事再做下一件事，我更喜歡同時進行多項工作。

Answer 7-2

I find it much more interesting to multi-task, and I find that I accomplish more than if I try to handle one problem at a time.

我覺得多工任務更有意思，而且比起一次只做一項工作，我在同時進行多工任務時能完成更多事。

Answer 7-3

I find that I multi-task far better than single-task. When I tackle one problem at a time, I tend to dwell on the solution, but when I have multiple things to accomplish, I am able to focus on the most accurate solution right away.

我發現我同時進行多項任務比單項任務效率更高。當我一次只應對一個問題的時候，我會執著於一個解決方案；而當我同時進行多項任務時，我能立刻集中在最佳的解決方案。

▶▶ 單字片語練功坊

1. accuracy　*n. [U]* 正確性
2. compromise　*vt.* 妥協、和解；連累、危害
3. affect　*vt.* 影響
4. work out　使...成功
5. supervisor　*n. [C]* 上司；管理人
6. figure out　理解；解決
7. bring… to someone's attention　讓某人注意到...
8. boundary　*n. [C]* 界線
9. temp　*n. [C]* 臨時工作
10. have no difficulty V-ing　做...沒有困難
11. multi-task　*vi.* 進行多工任務
12. on a daily basis　每天地

13. atmosphere   *n. [C]* 氣氛
14. appreciate   *vt.* 欣賞；感謝
15. accomplish   *vt.* 完成；達成
16. tackle   *vt.* 處理；應付
17. tend to   有...的傾向
18. solution   *n. [C]* 解決方法

date: /   /

零售客戶服務
Retail Customer Service track 040

>> **Q1** **What is customer service?**
什麼是客戶服務？

Answer 1-1

Customer service is more than waiting on customers. It includes trying your best to make sure that the customer is satisfied.

客戶服務不僅僅是服務客戶。它包括盡你最大的努力去讓客戶滿意。

Answer 1-2

Customer service is being friendly and helpful to customers.

客戶服務就是對客戶友善並協助客戶。

Answer 1-3

Customer service is helping customers satisfy the need that brought them into the store.

客戶服務是協助滿足他們的需求，正是這些需求把他們帶入商場的。

>> **Q2 What is good customer service?**
什麼是好的客戶服務？

Answer 2-1

Good customer service means having thorough knowledge of your inventory and experience with your products, and being able to help customers make the best choices for themselves.

好的客戶服務意味著清楚地知道庫存情況，以及豐富的商品經驗，並且能夠幫助顧客做出對自己最好的選擇。

Answer 2-2

Good customer service means helping customers efficiently, in a friendly manner.

好的客戶服務是有效率地、並友善地幫助客戶。

Answer 2-3

Good customer service is treating customers with a friendly, helpful attitude.

好的客戶服務就是以友善、有用的態度去對待客戶。

Chapter 3

▶▶Q3　Why do customers shop at this store?
為什麼客戶要在這家商場購物？

Answer 3-1

People shop here because the selection of merchandise is extensive, and the quality is excellent. The associates are always helpful and friendly. I would love the opportunity to be a part of such a well-run organization.

客戶在此購物是因為這裡的商品選擇範圍廣，而且品質非常好。服務人員樂於幫助而且態度友好。我希望能夠有機會成為這個優秀組織中的一員。

Answer 3-2

Customers can find terrific bargains, especially with the assistance of the helpful and friendly sales associates.

客戶在這裡能夠找到划算的商品，尤其是還有友善又有幫助的銷售人員幫助。

Answer 3-3

Because this store offers customer service and products that are superior to others in the area.

因為這個商場提供在這個區域中，最優秀的客戶服務以及商品。

Answer 3-4

This store offers terrific value in its selection and pricing.

因為這裡的商品物美價廉。

>> Q4　Why do you work in customer service?
你為什麼要做客戶服務工作？

Answer 4-1

I like dealing with customers, even though there are many irritating and irate customers. However, I do realize that my job depends on customers' satisfaction, and therefore I make a big effort to satisfy them.

我喜歡與客戶接洽，即使有一些讓人火大或是生氣的客戶。然而，我了解我的工作是以客戶的滿意為基礎，因此我很努力讓他們滿意。

Answer 4-2

I love dealing with customers. I really enjoy the interaction with people and find no problem answering even the most trivial questions. I get a deep sense of satisfaction when solving problems or helping customers out in one way or another.

我喜歡與客戶接洽。我很喜歡與人交流互動，很擅長回答問題，即使是十分瑣碎的小問題。當我解決了問題或用任何方式幫助客戶的時候，我得到一種深層的滿足感。

❯❯ Q5 A customer leaves without paying for gas. What would you do?
如果有個顧客沒有付汽油錢就走了。你會怎麼做？

Answer 5-1

Hopefully, I would have seen the license plate, and we could find who they were and remind them that they forgot to pay. It's possible that it was an honest error, and that the customer will return on his own to pay the bill.

希望我能看到車牌，這樣就能查出顧客是誰，並提醒他們忘了付款。可能只是一時疏忽，顧客會自己回來付款。

Answer 5-2

If it was a regular customer I was familiar with, I would make a note to my co-workers to mention it to him the next time he came in.

如果是個我熟悉的常客，我會告知我的同事，在他下次光臨時向他提起。

Answer 5-3

Sometimes people are in such a rush that they forget to complete the transaction. I would try to get the license plate, or a good description of the car and driver, and notify the manager.

有時人比較匆忙而忘了完成交易。我會試著查到車牌號碼，或是對汽車和司機詳細描述，然後通知經理。

>> **Q6** **A co-worker is rude to customers. What would you do?**
如果你的同事對顧客很粗魯。你會怎麼做？

Answer 6-1

That would depend on what kind of a rapport I had with him. If I felt comfortable, I would probably mention that being rude is probably going to be bad for him in the long run, since unhappy customers reflect badly on the sales associates. Otherwise, I would mention to the supervisor what I had witnessed, and let him handle it.

那要看我與他的關係如何。如果我覺得可以的話，我可能會說對顧客粗魯對他自己的長遠發展是不利的，因為顧客不開心就會影響銷售人員。不然的話，我會告訴經理我所目擊的情況，並讓他處理。

Answer 6-2

I would try to set a good example, by being courteous and helpful to customers and my co-workers.

我會試著做個好榜樣，禮貌又樂於幫助顧客和我的同事。

Answer 6-3

I'd try to get friendly with him, and see if there was something going on that was making him unhappy. Maybe he would just want to talk, and his attitude would improve.

我會試著和他用友好的態度，看看有什麼事情讓他不高興了。也許他只是想要傾訴，這樣他的態度就會有所改善。

Chapter 3

Answer 6-4

If it only happened when the supervisor was gone, I would definitely call it to his attention. I wouldn't want to be a snitch, but a store's reputation depends largely on its customer service, and rude sales associates can have a negative impact on that reputation.

如果只發生在經理不在的時候，我一定會讓經理注意到。我不是想要當告密的人，只是商場的名譽大部分要靠它的客戶服務，而粗魯的銷售人員會給商場的名譽帶來負面的影響。

>> **Q7 The credit card machine is broken. What do you say to the customers?**
刷卡機壞了。你會怎麼向顧客說？

Answer 7-1

I would offer to hold the merchandise for 24 to 48 hours, and offer to call when the machine is fixed, so they can return for it.

我會主動提出替顧客保留商品24到48個小時，當刷卡機修好，就會打電話通知他們，這樣他們就可以回來購買商品了。

Answer 7-2

I'm so sorry that the machine is down. Usually it's back up in a little while. Can I hold the merchandise while you do some other shopping, and you can come back in a bit for it?

很抱歉刷卡機壞了。一般來說應該一小會兒就能好了。我能否幫您先

保留商品，您去其他地方先逛一逛，然後一會兒回來購買可以嗎？

Answer 7-3

We also take cash and checks, and there is an ATM on the corner. I'm sorry for the inconvenience, but if you'd like, I can hold the merchandise while you go to the ATM.

我們也收現金和支票，轉角那兒有台自動提款機。為您帶來不便我很抱歉，如果您願意，您可以去自動提款機領錢，在此期間，我可以為您先保留商品。

》Q8　A customer wants to return a package of food that is open and half gone. What will you do?
　　如果有顧客想退一包已經打開並且只剩一半的食品。你會怎麼做？

Answer 8-1

The company policy would be important to know here. Some food companies stand behind their product 100%. You could feel confident giving the customer another package, then returning the opened one for a refund for the store.

首先了解公司在這個部份的政策很重要。有的食品公司百分之百保證產品的售後。你就可以有信心地換一包給顧客，將打開的那包退貨給公司。

Answer 8-2

Clearly, this is a delicate judgment call. Generally speaking, I would take the package back and replace it with another, unless I was certain that the customer was really trying to take advantage of the situation. Sometimes taking a small loss can pay off in customer loyalty.

很顯然，這要做出精妙的判斷。一般來說，我會將那包收回，並給顧客更換一包，除非我確定顧客是想占便宜。有時吃點小虧能換來顧客的信賴。

⟩⟩ Q9 What is most important — a good product or friendly, fast service?
優質產品和友善迅速的服務哪一個最重要？

Answer 9-1

Both are extremely important. A good product is essential, but without the customer service to back it up, there is no reason for someone to buy it here as opposed to somewhere else or online.

兩者都很重要。好的產品是基礎，但如果沒有客戶服務來支援，沒有理由人們要在這裡購買，而不是去別的地方或是網路上。

Answer 9-2

Fast, friendly service can make a bargain product much more attractive to customers.

友善、迅速的服務能讓划算的產品變得更加吸引顧客。

Answer 9-3

A superior product will speak for itself, and friendly, efficient customer service is what will set us apart from the competition.

一個優秀的產品會替自己說話，而友好、有效率的客戶服務能夠讓我們在競爭中與別人不同。

>> **Q10** **You are scheduled to leave at 6 p.m. Your replacement worker doesn't show up. What would you do?**
你應該在下午6點下班。但你的接班同事沒有來，你會怎麼做？

Answer 10-1

I would call my supervisor to let her know, and would stay until I was sure the selling floor was covered.
我會打電話給上司告訴她，而且我會待到確定賣場有人接班了。

Answer 10-2

I would try to call him to see when he would be coming in, and I would make arrangements to stay until he arrived.
我會試著給他打電話，看他什麼時候能來，我會做些安排然後留下來，直到他抵達。

>> **Q11** **A customer complains that the coffee tastes terrible. What would you do?**
有顧客投訴咖啡不好喝。你會怎麼做？

Answer 11-1

I would take her complaint seriously. I would take some from the dispenser that hers came from, and smell and taste it. If it seemed off, I would make a fresh brew. If it seemed fine, I would offer her the option of trying another brew, as this one may not have been to her taste.

我會認真處理她的投訴。我會取一些和她杯中一樣的咖啡來聞聞並品嘗。如果咖啡不新鮮，我會重新煮新鮮的。如果咖啡沒什麼問題，我會讓顧客選擇換一種，因為可能她喝的這種不合她的口味。

Answer 11-2

I would suggest that perhaps this particular brew was not to her taste, and offer her the option of choosing another.

我會建議說，可能這一種咖啡不合她的口味，然後讓她可以換一種。

Answer 11-3

I would offer to make a fresh pot for the customer, and replace her coffee with a fresh one.

我會重新煮一壺咖啡，然後給顧客換一杯新鮮的。

》 單字片語練功坊

1. wait on　服務
2. inventory　n. [C] 存貨清單
3. attitude　n. [C] 態度
4. selection　n. [U] 選擇
5. extensive　adj. 廣大的；廣泛的
6. quality　n. [U] 品質
7. associate　n. [C] 同事
8. opportunity　n. [C] 機會

9. assistance　*n. [U]* 協助

10. superior　*adj.* 較好的；優秀的

11. deal with　處理；應付

12. depend on　依靠；信賴

13. effort　*n. [C]* 努力

14. sense of satisfaction　滿足感

15. error　*n. [C]* 錯誤

16. in a rush　急忙之中

17. transaction　*n. [C]* 交易；買賣

18. notify　*vt.* 通知；告知

19. in the long run　長期來說；最終

20. reflect on　反映在......

21. set an example　立下範例

22. reputation　*n. [C]* 名譽；名聲

23. impact　*n. [C]* 影響

24. merchandise　*n. [U]* 商品；貨物

25. refund　*n. [C]* 退款

26. replace　*vt.* 取代；替換

27. take advantage of　占...的好處

28. pay off　成功；有成效

29. essential　*adj.* 必要的；不可缺少的

30. back up　支持

31. as opposed to　相對於......

兼職工作 Part-time Job track 041

≫ Q1　What days and hours are you available to work?
你哪些時間可以上班？

Answer 1-1

I'm available during school hours, while my children are at school. In other words, from 9 a.m. to 3 p.m. Monday through Friday. I can work some weekends, too.

我孩子在每週一到週五的上午九點到下午三點上學，這段時間我可以來上班。有時週末我也能工作。

Answer 1-2

(If you're a student, you'll need to share your class schedule, and any labs, with your supervisor)

I have classes Tuesday and Thursday until 4 p.m., and a lab that meets every other Wednesday from 5 p.m. to 7 p.m., but I'm flexible about working any other hours you have available.

（如果你是一名學生，你需要把課程表及實驗室課程告知你的上司）

週二到週四我有課，上到下午四點，週三下午的五點到七點有實驗室的課，但其他任何您可以的時間我都可以來上班。

❯❯ Q2 Do you have any activities that would prevent you from working your schedule?
你有什麼活動會讓你不按照計畫來安排時間嗎？

Answer 2-1

I participate every year in a run to raise money for my favorite charity, but I'll know the date well in advance and would let you know I need that day off.

每年我會參加一項跑步比賽，為我最喜歡的慈善機構募款，但我會提前知道比賽日期，並會讓您知道我需要那天請假。

Answer 2-2

I'm in the Students' Union at school, but our practices are typically early in the morning or later in the day, so they shouldn't impact my schedule.

我是學生會的一員，但我們的活動一般在早晨或是傍晚，所以不會影響到我的時程表。

Answer 2-3

I spend a week during the winter vacationing with my family in Kenting every year, but I can schedule that based on the busy times at work.

每年冬天我會和家人一起在墾丁度假一周，但我會根據工作的忙碌時段來安排這趟旅行的時間。

Chapter 3

Answer 2-4

I volunteer at the hospital every Saturday morning from 9 a.m. till noon, and other than that my schedule is flexible.

每週六從上午九點到中午，我會在一家醫院做義工，除了這個之外我的時程表很彈性。

>> **Q3   Would you prefer full-time employment to part-time if a job were available?**
如果有工作職缺的話，你會選擇做全職員工，而不是兼職嗎？

Answer 3-1

Right now, my education, family, and children prevent me from considering full-time employment, but I wouldn't rule it out at some point in the future.

目前來說，因為我的學業、家庭和孩子使我不能考慮全職工作，但我不排除將來也許可以。

Answer 3-2

What is important to me is that I enjoy the work and the people I'm working with. I have many interests, and having a part-time job allows me the time to pursue them.

對我來說，重要的是我喜歡我的工作和一起工作的人。我有很多興趣，而從事兼職工作能給我時間去追求這些興趣。

Chapter 3

▶▶ Q4 How would you describe the pace at which you work?
你會怎麼描述你的工作節奏？

Answer 4-1

I work very efficiently, so I accomplish a lot in a short amount of time.
我工作非常有效率，所以我能在很短的時間內完成很多事。

Answer 4-2

I'm terrific at multi-tasking, so I typically get all my work done ahead of schedule.
我很善於同時進行多項任務，所以一般而言我能提前完成工作。

Answer 4-3

I am very focused on my work, and consequently, I am able to work quickly.
我很專注於工作，因此，我工作起來很快。

Answer 4-4

I keep a steady pace and check my work as I go along, to prevent mistakes from snowballing.
我工作步調很穩定，並且一邊進行一邊檢查工作，以防有錯誤愈來愈嚴重。

Answer 4-5

Because I am very organized, I am able to accomplish a lot in a limited amount of time.

因為我做事很有條理，所以我能在有限的時間裡完成很多事。

≫ Q5　What do you know about this company?
你對這個公司了解多少？

Answer 5-1

Your company's products are the highest rated in the industry.
貴公司的產品在這個產業中是最佳的。

Answer 5-2

This company has the reputation for excellent customer service.
貴公司因為極佳的客戶服務而擁有很好的名譽。

Answer 5-3

This company was awarded an industry-wide commendation for the work done to help the victims of the 921 earthquake.
貴公司因為在921大地震中幫助受難者的義行，而在此行業中深受讚譽。

≫ Q6　What applicable experience do you have?
你有哪些有用的經驗？

Answer 6-1

I have very similar experience to what you're looking for. In my current position, I hold the responsibilities that I'd have if I were to be offered this job.

我的經驗和您所需要的非常相似。在我現在的工作中，我所負責的事項和這份工作要求的是一樣的。

Answer 6-2

I have several years of office experience.

我有幾年的辦公室經驗。

Answer 6-3

At my last job, my responsibilities included many of those required for this position.

在我上一個工作中，我負責的很多事情也是這份工作所要求的。

》》Q7　What are you looking for in your next job? What is important to you?

你在下一份工作中想要尋找的是什麼？什麼對你來說比較重要？

Answer 7-1

I'm looking for an interesting position with flexible hours. It's important to me that I find my work intellectually stimulating.

我想要尋找的是一份工時彈性的職位。我認為工作能夠激發我的理性思維是很重要的。

Answer 7-2

I'm looking for a position that will be able to accommodate my school schedule. My education is my priority right now, but I would like to work with a nice bunch of people.

我想要找一份能和我學校時間安排調和的工作。當前我最重要的任務是學業，但我也想和一些友善的人一起工作。

Answer 7-3

I'd like my next job to be challenging, one that will let me use my education and experience. It's important to me to continue learning and exercise my problem-solving skills.

我希望我下一份工作能有挑戰性，能讓我運用知識和經驗。對我來說，能夠不斷學習，並鍛鍊解決問題的能力是很重要的。

》Q8　What will you do if you don't get this position?
如果你沒有獲得這個職位，你會怎麼做？

Answer 8-1

I will continue looking in this field for another part-time position that will fit my schedule and goals.

我會繼續在這個領域尋找能夠適合我學校時間安排，以及符合目標的兼職工作。

Answer 8-2

I will consider broadening my search to include some different industries hiring part-time people.

我會考慮擴大我的應徵範圍，包括有僱用兼職人員的不同產業。

Answer 8-3

I really feel like this would be a good fit for me, so I'm hoping I won't have to think too much about that.

我真的認為這份工作非常適合我，所以我希望我不需要思考這個問題。

》》單字片語練功坊

1. available *adj.* 可用的；有效的
2. participate in 參與；加入
3. in advance 提前地
4. impact *vt.* 影響
5. flexible *adj.* 彈性的；靈活的
6. employment *n. [U]* 僱用；受僱
7. rule out 排除
8. pursue *vt.* 追求
9. ahead of schedule 比原本預定時間提前
10. consequently *adv.* 因此
11. snowball *vi.* 像雪球一樣地增大
12. award *vt.* 授予；給獎
13. commendation *n. [C]* 表揚；稱讚
14. responsibility *n. [C]* 責任
15. perfectionist *n. [C]* 完美主義者
16. punctual *adj.* 準時的
17. compel *vt.* 強迫；使不得不
18. intellectually *adv.* 智力上的
19. stimulating *adj.* 有刺激性的
20. accommodate *vt.* 使適應；使符合
21. priority *n. [C]* 優先；優先事項
22. broaden *vt.* 擴大；加寬

📁 銷售業務 Sales track 042

》》Q1　What interests you about selling to customers?
關於賣東西給顧客，哪一點吸引你？

Answer 1

I enjoy talking to the customer and finding out exactly what they are looking for. I like the challenge of meeting the customer's needs, making useful suggestions and making sure the customer leaves satisfied.

我喜歡和顧客溝通，並找出他們想要買的東西。我喜歡滿足客戶需求的挑戰、向他們提出有用的建議、並保證他們滿意地離開。

》》Q2　Have you consistently met your sales goals?
你總是能達到自己的銷售目標嗎？

Answer 2-1

I have met or exceeded my personal and professional sales goals consistently over the past 10 years.

在過去的十年中，我總是能夠達到或超過我的個人目標以及職業目標。

Answer 2-2

I have always met or exceeded my professional sales goals, and most often my personal ones too, especially in the last few years. I think I have learned to set my personal goals at an attainable level; very high, but not unreachable.

我總是能夠達到或超過我的職業銷售目標，對於個人目標通常也是如此，尤其是在過去這幾年當中。我認為我學會了如何設定能達成的個人目標；目標很高，但並非無法達成。

Answer 2-3

The only time I wasn't able to meet my professional sales goals was at a company where my supervisor set the goals extremely high, and none of the salespeople in our department were able to achieve them. Setting the goals so high was his method of keeping us motivated, and unfortunately it worked to demoralize the team instead. I have always at least met my personal goals, and I work very hard to exceed them.

我只有一次沒能達到我的銷售目標，當時我公司的上司把目標訂得特別高，我們部門沒有一個銷售員能夠達到。把目標訂得高是他用來激勵我們的方法，但不幸的是這反而打消了我們的團隊士氣。平時我至少總能達到我的個人目標，我非常努力工作來超越目標。

➤➤ Q3　Do you prefer a long or short sales cycle?
你偏好短的銷售週期還是長的銷售週期？

Answer 3-1

I think there are interesting points to both types of sales. I like a longer sales cycle, as it gives me time to get to know the customer, and spend time educating them about the benefits and uses of the product. Shorter cycles are more intense, since you typically don't have the luxury of too much personal knowledge of the customer, or the time for lengthy explanations. You need to hit the high priority topics rather quickly.

我認為這兩種銷售模式各有令人關注的點。我喜歡較長的銷售週期，因為這能給我時間來了解客戶，讓我花時間教育他們產品的好處和用途。較短的銷售週期工作較緊繃，因為你通常無法對客戶有太多的個人了解，也沒有時間進行耗時的說明。你需要迅速地挑出最重要的點說明。

Answer 3-2

I prefer a longer sales cycle, because the pace can be adjusted depending on the individual client you are dealing with. Some clients like to have a lot of information about a product right up front, are knowledgeable, and have a lot of technical questions. Others are more interested in the personal benefits of a product; with a longer cycle, I have the time to spend letting them know about the features that make this the right product for them.

我喜好較長的銷售週期，因為節奏可以根據所面對的客戶來進行調整。有的客戶喜歡獲得大量關於產品的資訊、是有知識的、會提出很多技術性的問題。而有的客戶則更注重產品能為他們帶來的好處；有較長的銷售週期，我就有時間讓他們了解產品特色，正是這些特色使產品符合他們的需求。

Answer 3-3

I really enjoy the quicker pace of a shorter sales cycle. I like to get right to the point about my product's features and benefits, and showcase the reasons why it's the best choice for the customer. I'm knowledgeable about what I am selling, and ready with answers to any questions a customer may have.

我喜歡較短的銷售週期較快的節奏。我喜歡直接切入主題，就是產品的特性和好處，並向他們展示為什麼這就是最好的選擇。我對我所銷售的產品很清楚，並隨時能夠回答顧客可能提出的任何問題。

》》Q4　How did you land your most successful sale? 你是如何完成最成功的一次銷售？

Answer 4-1

My most successful sale was one where I had taken over a customer from another salesperson who had to leave suddenly. I immediately contacted the person and let him know the situation. I knew that my colleague was having a difficult time getting the client to commit to the purchase of a large motor home. But when I was given the opportunity to take over the sale, I was able to give the customer some reflection time, and was ultimately able to close the sale.

我最成功的一次銷售是，我從另一位突然離職的銷售員接手客戶。我立刻聯繫顧客，告訴他這個情況。我知道我同事不是很順利，在讓他承諾買下大型露營車方面。但當我有機會接過這筆銷售時，我給了顧客一些考慮的時間，最後完成了銷售。

Answer 4-2

I would say that my most successful sales have followed a similar pattern. Once the customer has expressed interest in the product, I make myself available to answer any questions they may have. Next, I try to fill them in on the details they may not be familiar with; for example, features, benefits, etc. I believe that when a customer is making a purchase, especially a large one, they like to have time to fully understand what features the item has, and what makes one company preferable to deal with than another. By representing a company with a superior product and a high level of customer support, I am confident in offering a fair price, and I have been very successful at landing most of my sales.

我會說我最成功的銷售基本上都是遵循一套模式。一旦顧客表現出對產品感興趣，我會讓自己能夠回答他們可能提出的各種問題。接著，我會向他們介紹他們可能不熟悉的細節，比如說特性、好處等等。我相信當顧客在消費購買，尤其是大筆金額時，他們想要花時

間來徹底了解商品的特性，並會貨比三家。作為具有優質商品和高水準客戶支援的公司代表，我有信心能夠提供合理的價格，並且我大部分的銷售都相當成功。

Answer 4-3

I have been very fortunate to have met many interesting people in my career in sales. One of the sales which I would consider my most successful was an international sale of a large number of books which had been returned after a major retailer closed. Through my contacts, I learned of an English Language bookstore in a small suburb of Delhi, and I was able to offer the owner a terrific deal, which helped out my company tremendously, by not having to re-stock the items.

我很幸運，在我的銷售職涯中遇到了很多有意思的人。我認為我最成功的銷售之一，是一筆大量書籍的國際訂單，這個訂單是一個歇業的大型零售商退貨的。通過我的人脈，我知道德里郊區有一間英語書店，並提供書店老闆一個優惠價格，這大大地幫助了我的公司，不需要把書重新入庫存。

>> **Q5 How would your colleagues describe you?**
你的同事會如何描述你？

Answer 5-1

My colleagues describe me as tenacious, detail-oriented, and successful.

我的同事說我是一個頑強、注意細節、而且成功的人。

Answer 5-2

I think most of my colleagues would describe me as a people person. I really enjoy the opportunity I have as a salesperson to meet with and learn about lots of interesting people from many different places.

我想大部分同事都會說我是一個很會與人相處的人。我真的很高興我能作為一名銷售員，有機會和很多地方有趣的人相處並學習。

Answer 5-3

My colleagues would describe me as very organized and detail-oriented. I am one of those people who have their pens lined up in their desk drawer. If I weren't so organized, I wouldn't be able to service the volume of clients that I can.

我的同事會說我是個很有條理的人，而且很注意細節。我會把筆整齊地排列好放在抽屜裡。如果我不是這麼有條理的話，我就不會有今天這麼多的客戶了。

》Q6   How would your former supervisor describe you?
       你之前的上司會怎麼描述你？

Answer 6-1

She would describe me as a person who leaves no loose ends. I have often been complimented on my attention to detail.

她會說我是個做事有始有終的人。我常因為注意細節受到讚賞。

Answer 6-2

My former supervisor would say that I work well as a part of team, as well as being motivated on my own. At that particular company, it was important to be able to keep all the team members informed, as we worked collaboratively on many sales. It was an interesting environment, and I found it enjoyable and challenging.

我的前任上司會說，我在團隊中工作優秀，獨自工作也很有動力。在那間公司，及時把訊息傳達給所有團隊成員是十分重要的，因為我們在許多銷售上都要共同合作。那是一個很有意思的工作環境，在那裡工作很愉悅也很有挑戰性。

Answer 6-3

He would describe me as a self starter. We were responsible for our sales from first contact to close, and worked alone and independently most of the time. There were some experienced salespeople who had a difficult time with the lack of structure there, but I found it satisfying to have that kind of autonomy.

他會說我工作獨立。我們負責從銷售開始的接觸到銷售結束，而且大部分時間是獨自獨立工作。有些有經驗的銷售員覺得這種缺乏組織的方式很難適應，但我很滿意這種自治的方式。

Chapter 3

▶▶ Q7　What are your long-term career goals?
你長遠的職涯目標是什麼？

Answer 7-1

Long term, I see myself as a Senior Sales Director at a large wholesaler or retailer. I really enjoy being in sales, and I believe that I have the ability to manage a large, successful sales team.

我的長期目標是在一家大型的批發商或是零售商，擔任資深銷售指導。我真的很喜歡銷售行業，並且我相信我有能力管理一個大型的成功銷售團隊。

Answer 7-2

I am interested in all aspects of the retail market, and I see myself in the long term spending some time working in a variety of roles.

我對零售市場所有方面都很感興趣，所以我的長期目標是能夠在這個領域上，不同的職位都做一段時間的工作。

Answer 7-3

I expect to remain in sales throughout my career, moving from direct sales eventually into a management role.

我希望我的職涯一直在銷售領域工作，從直接銷售最終能做到管理階層。

≫ Q8　What are your strengths and weaknesses?
你有哪些優勢和劣勢？

Answer 8-1

I would say that my greatest strength is my ability to follow through. My greatest weakness is my tendency to over-think a situation. I sometimes take too much time to strategize on a sale, and find in the end that my initial plan was the one that was the best.

我想說我最大的優勢是能夠堅持到底。我最大的劣勢是我常常對於一個情況考慮過多。我有時候在銷售策略的制訂上花太多時間，最後發現一開始的方案是最好的。

Answer 8-2

My greatest strength is my organizational ability. I like to plan out the sales cycle to the letter and follow it through. My greatest weakness is related to my greatest strength, because I would say that when my plan needs to change, I can be a little bit inflexible.

我最大的長處在於我的組織能力。我喜歡將銷售循環的計畫做得十分詳細，然後根據計畫做事。我最大的弱點和我最大的長處有關，因為如果我的計畫需要修改，我有點不夠彈性。

Answer 8-3

My greatest strength is my ability to think on my feet. I am very flexible in my approach to sales and am able to work with many different kinds of customers at once. My weakness is that sometimes I don't plan things out as well as I should and end up reacting to things as they come up.

我最大的長處是我反應迅速。我用於銷售的方法靈活，而且能迅速和不同的顧客應對。我的短處是有時我對事情做計畫做得不夠好，只好事情發生的時候再想對策。

▶▶ Q9　What do you find most rewarding about being in sales?
什麼最讓你覺得做銷售是值得的？

Answer 9-1

I really enjoy making contacts and spending time talking with people. The most rewarding part of being in sales, for me, is the time spent with customers, helping them make the right decision about a product.

我真的很喜歡與人接觸，花時間和人交談。對我而言，在銷售部門工作最值得的部分是，和顧客相處的時間，幫助他們對於產品做出正確的決定。

Answer 9-2

I think the most rewarding thing about sales is providing customers with the best service possible. I pride myself on making sure that a customer knows about the product they are purchasing, and has the ability to use it to its fullest potential.

我認為關於銷售最值得的是，提供最佳的服務給顧客。我很自豪

一點，確保顧客了解他們購買的產品，並且有能力物盡其用地使用產品。

Answer 9-3

The most rewarding thing about being in sales, for me, is the satisfaction of helping a customer to realize their goals. Once I had a customer who was restructuring her children's rooms and needed to place a large number of books in the rooms. We had a great time making selections together, and she was really pleased with the variety I was able to help her select.

對我來說，在銷售部門工作最值得的是，幫助顧客實現他們的目標所帶來的滿足感。有一次，我遇到一位顧客在重新布置她孩子們的房間，需要在房間裡放很多書。我們很愉快地一起選擇，她很滿意我幫她挑的各類書籍。

▶▶ Q10　What do you know about this company?
你對這家公司的了解有多少？

Answer 10-1

I know that this company is the number one widget wholesaler in Taiwan, with a growing overseas presence in Europe and the US. Additionally, your sales in the US have grown by 25% in the last three years, and your widget sales are beginning to outpace the American competition. Domestically, your sales continue to grow steadily, even through the economic downturn, and subsequent plateau, that your competition has faced.

我知道這家公司是全台灣第一名的飾品批發商，在歐洲和美國的能見度也不斷提高。另外，你們在美國的銷量在過去三年中增加了25%，開始超越美國本土的競爭者。在國內，你們的銷量也不斷穩定成長，即使和同業一起經歷了經濟危機及緊接來的經濟平穩。

Answer 10-2

This company was rated one of "Taiwan's Best Small Companies" in 2012, and has shown consistent growth in the market. Your sales have surpassed expectations, and your innovative products and sales techniques have made you one of the most desirable companies to work for in Taiwan.

這家公司在2012年「台灣最佳小型企業」中榜上有名，並且在市場上持續成長。你們的銷售量超出預期，你們擁有創新的產品和銷售技巧，這些使得你們成為台灣最想進入工作的公司之一。

Answer 10-3

In my research about this company, I discovered that you had started out over 100 years ago as a small brick and mortar retailer in Tainan. As a family-owned business, you had the savvy to grow in unique ways, and when the opportunity arose to go public in 1993, the decision was clear. Since then, the management has continued to make aggressive decisions, keeping your business in the forefront of its competition.

我對貴公司做了研究，我發現你們有超過100年的歷史，從台南一家實體零售商起家。作為一個家族企業，你們懂得以獨特的方式發

展，當1993年有機會上市時，你們果斷做出了決定。在那之後，管理階層持續做出積極的決定，保持貴公司成為競爭中的佼佼者。

》Q11　What do you least like about being in sales?
銷售中你最不喜歡的部分是什麼？

Answer 11-1

I really enjoy being in sales, and I try to look at the whole package when assessing my likes and dislikes. While sometimes there is a difficult customer, or a company who doesn't stand behind their product the way I'd like, the vast majority of the time I am happy to help my customers, and am proud of the companies I represent.

我真的很喜歡銷售這份工作，我試著從全面的角度去看事情，當我評價喜歡和不喜歡的事情時。雖然有時候會遇到難對付的顧客，或者產品售後服務不如期待的公司，但大部分情況下，我很樂於幫助我的顧客，也為我所代表的公司感到驕傲。

Answer 11-2

The one thing that I don't like about being in sales is when I feel pressured to make a sale, just to make a sale, regardless of whether the customer is going to be happy with the product. I have found that, more often than not, that's not a good way to conduct business, and a company's reputation, as well as the salesman's, can become damaged by the practice.

對於銷售我不喜歡有一點是，我受到壓力必須完成銷售，只是完

成銷售，不管顧客是否會滿意這項產品。我發現通常情況下，這不是一個做生意的好方法，公司和銷售員的名譽都可能因此作法而受損。

>> **Q12 What interests you most about this sales position?**
關於這份銷售的職位，什麼最吸引你？

Answer 12-1

I'm an avid amateur golfer, and I find your company's products to be incredibly easy to use, and helpful to the average person. I believe selling something that I personally enjoy using so much makes me even more effective as a salesperson.

我是個狂熱的高爾夫業餘愛好者，而我發現貴公司的產品非常易於使用，對於一般人來說很有幫助。我相信賣一些我自己真心喜歡的東西，能使我作為銷售員更有效率。

Answer 12-2

I have worked in this territory for many years, and would welcome the opportunity to utilize my experience selling a superior product such as this.

我在這個領域中工作很多年了，我希望能有機會用我的經驗去銷售一些像這樣的高品質產品。

Answer 12-3

The opportunity to travel internationally and utilize my

experience in sales is what interests me most about this position.

這個職務最吸引我的地方是，有機會到國外出差，並運用我的銷售經驗。

≫ Q13　What is more important: a quality product or excellent customer service?
高品質產品和優秀的客戶服務哪個更重要？

Answer 13-1

I believe that the two go hand in hand. You are not doing a service to your customers by selling an inferior product. I make sure that the products that I represent are all of high quality and are of good value, which gives me the confidence that I am providing my customers with the best possible customer service.

我相信這兩者緊密相關。如果銷售品質不好的產品，就不算是服務顧客。我要確保我所代表的產品都是高品質、有價值的，這能給我自信，我對顧客提供最好的客戶服務。

Answer 13-2

The quality product comes first. When you are able to provide a consistently high quality product, you are providing the customer with the most important aspect of customer service: a superior product experience.

高品質的產品更重要。當你能一直提供高品質的產品，你就是在為顧客提供客戶服務中最重要的面向，那就是優質的產品體驗。

Answer 13-3

Customer service is the most important aspect of sales. Without friendly, knowledgeable service, no product can sell itself.

客戶服務是銷售中最重要的面向。如果沒有友善、介紹詳盡的服務，就不可能賣出產品。

>> **Q14   What makes you a good salesperson?**
      你為什麼是一名優秀的銷售員？

Answer 14-1

I'm an ambitious person, and that helps me in sales. I really like to make sure that my customers are thoroughly informed, and that I provide the best possible service. I feel like I've done a good job when I have made a sale that required using all my talents.

我是一個目標遠大的人，這點幫助了我的銷售工作。我真心想要確保顧客徹底地被告知產品資訊，並確保我提供了最好的服務。當我用所有的才能完成一筆銷售，我就覺得我做得很好。

Answer 14-2

I think that my patience helps me be a good salesperson. I find that I have made some of my best sales when I have taken the time to let the customers weigh their decision carefully, ask as many questions as they wished, and not put too much pressure on them.

我認為我的耐心幫助我成為優秀的銷售員。我發現我完成了一些最成功的銷售，都是我讓顧客仔細考慮他們的決定，讓他們儘量發問，不要給他們太多壓力。

》Q15　What motivates you?
是什麼給你動力？

Answer 15-1

I am motivated by a challenge. I enjoy spending the time to showcase a product and help the customer to understand the benefits to them.

是挑戰給了我動力。我喜歡花時間去展示產品，並幫助客戶了解產品能帶給他們的好處。

Answer 15-2

What motivates me most is money. I enjoy making large sales, seeking out new clients, and growing my department's earnings.

最能給我動力的是金錢。我喜歡完成大筆的銷售、尋找新的客戶、增長我在部門內的銷售比例。

Answer 15-3

I am motivated by innovation. I like to try different things, and I love being in sales, because every customer brings the opportunity for a new approach.

是創新給了我動力。我喜歡嘗試不同的東西，我喜歡做銷售，因為每一個客戶都給了我機會用不同的方式來工作。

Chapter 3

▶▶ Q16　Are you comfortable making cold calls?
你擅長電話推銷嗎？

Answer 16-1

Absolutely. I enjoy reaching out to people with new products and ideas.

當然。我喜歡向人們介紹新產品和新觀念。

Answer 16-2

I am comfortable making cold calls. I have found that some of my most interesting sales have been the result of a cold call, to someone who was rather unsure of their interest in my product at our first meeting.

我擅長電話推銷。我發現最有意思的銷售都是電話推銷的成果，打給那些在第一次見面不確定自己對產品有沒有興趣的人。

Answer 16-3

I don't mind making cold calls, but I prefer to start my sales cycle with a customer who has shown some interest in the product.

我不介意通過電話推銷，但我更喜歡開始銷售循環，是和對產品感興趣的顧客。

▶▶ 單字片語練功坊

1. challenge　*n. [C]* 挑戰
2. suggestion　*n. [C]* 建議

3. make sure 確保；確定

4. exceed *vt.* 超過；勝過

5. attainable *adj.* 可達到的

6. extremely *adv.* 非常地；極

7. motivate *vt.* 給...動機；激勵

8. demoralize *vt.* 使士氣低落；使喪氣

9. benefit *n. [C]* 好處；益處

10. intense *adj.* 強烈的；劇烈的

11. feature *n. [C]* 特色

12. showcase *vt.* 展示；陳列

13. immediately *adv.* 立刻

14. commit to 做出保證；表態

15. purchase *n. [C]* 購買

16. take over 接管；接收

17. pattern *n. [C]* 模式

18. fill someone in on 讓某人知道...

19. detail *n. [C]* 細節

20. familiar with 對...熟悉

21. represent *vt.* 代表

22. land *vt.* 弄到；完成

23. retailer *n. [C]* 零售商

24. contact *n. [C]* 人脈

25. complement *vt.* 誇獎；讚美

26. structure *n. [C]* 結構；構造

27. autonomy *n. [U]* 自治

28. aspect　*n. [C]* 面向；觀點

29. initial　*adj.* 最初的；開始的

30. to the letter　不折不扣的；完全依照文字的

31. approach　*n. [C]* 方法；作法

32. rewarding　*adj.* 有報酬的；有益的

33. pride oneself on　以...自豪

34. potential　*n. [U]* 潛力；可能性

35. outpace　*vt.* 勝過；趕過

36. economic　*adj.* 經濟的

37. downturn　*n. [C]* 經濟衰退

38. subsequent　*adj.* 隨後的；後來的

39. surpass　*vt.* 超過；越過

40. aggressive　*adj.* 有進取精神的；有幹勁的

41. assess　*vt.* 評估；評價

42. regardless of　不管

43. amateur　*adj.* 業餘的

44. territory　*n. [C]* 領域；範圍

45. ambitious　*adj.* 有野心的；有企圖心的

46. put pressure on　給...壓力

47. feedback　*n. [U]* 回饋

48. financial　*adj.* 財務的

49. update　*vt.* 更新；提供新訊息

50. submit　*vt.* 提交；呈遞

管理人員 **Manager** track 043

》》**Q1　How would your co-workers describe you?**
你的同事是怎麼描述你的？

Answer 1

My co-workers will tell you that I am a team player and a colleague they can count on to pull his weight, whether it's a normal day or we're in a crunch.

我同事會告訴你，我是個團隊合作能力很強的人，是他們能依靠的同事，會盡自己的全力，無論是一般的日子還是緊要關頭的時候。

》》**Q2　What is your definition of success?**
你對成功的定義是什麼？

Answer 2

In my opinion, and as it relates to the workplace, success is a measurable variable. If you don't measure your accomplishments, success is lost. Success can be tied to everything you do each day. If I plan to accomplish three tasks before the end of the day and I do so, then I have been successful. Success simply means accomplishing what you set out to do within the parameters you specify, whether they be time, money, learning, or anything else.

我認為在工作職場上，成功是可量化的變數。如果你不量化自己的成就，成功就會消逝。成功可以跟你每天做的每件事綁在一起，如

果我計畫今天結束前完成三項任務並做到，那麼我就是成功的。簡單地說，成功是指，在你設定的參數內完成你想要完成的任務，參數可以是時間、金錢、學習或是任何其他事。

>> Q3　What is your definition of failure?
你對失敗的定義是什麼？

Answer 3

For starters, failure is an event and not a person. You only fail if you quit, and I'm not a quitter.

首先，失敗是一件事而不是一個人。只有你放棄了你才會失敗，而我不是一個會放棄的人。

>> Q4　What is your viewpoint of management?
你對管理的看法是什麼？

Answer 4

I believe the main goal of any management position is to get things done by evenly distributing the workload to the most qualified members of the team. They also make sure that each member of the team has all the resources and training that are necessary to complete the job. They are loyal and are always working in the best interests of the company. Their job is tough; they must evaluate employee performance, empower members of the team, and be able to identify those who are not pulling their own weight.

我認為，任何管理職位的主要任務都是把事情完成，透過將工作量

平均分配給團隊中最有資格的成員。他們也要確保團隊的每個成員得到完成工作所需的資源和培訓。他們是忠誠的，永遠為了公司的最佳利益而工作。他們的工作很困難，他們必須評價員工的表現、授權團隊成員，並能夠挑出那些沒有為公司盡力的人。

▶▶ Q5　Do you know who our competitors are?
你知道我們的競爭對手有哪些嗎？

Answer 5

Yes, I work for one of them, but I have always admired your company and have always wanted to work here.

我知道，我曾在貴公司的競爭對手公司裡工作，但一直仰慕貴公司，並想來到這裡工作。

▶▶ Q6　Do you feel that you are an organized person?
你認為自己是個有條理的人嗎？

Answer 6

Yes, I consider myself to be very well organized. Every day when I arrive at work, I check my email and messages. Then I plan out exactly what I am going to do that day. At the end of the day, I review my progress and plan for the following day.

是的，我認為自己很有條理。每天我一到公司，都會查閱電子郵件和訊息。接著詳細計畫一天的工作。工作結束時，我會回顧進度並為次日做計畫。

≫ Q7 How do you manage your time?
你是如何管理個人時間的？

Answer 7

I have found that if I don't create daily, weekly, and monthly goals, it seems like nothing ever gets done. I keep track of all my responsibilities and goals in spreadsheet and review them daily. When I am first assigned a task, I mark down how long I think it will take, when it needs to be completed, and how much time I will need to spend on it each day to complete the job on time. This helps me in so many ways, but mainly it keeps me on track with what is important. It also helps me from getting overbooked and promising more than I can deliver. Now, I can always deliver what I promise and be on time.

我發現如果我不制訂每日目標、每週目標和每月目標，似乎沒有事情可以完成。我用試算表來記錄我所有的職責和目標，並每日進行回顧。我會記下我開始接受某項任務的時間、預估完成所需的時間、必須完成的日期、以及每天需用多少時間來完成這項任務。這麼做在很多方面很有幫助，但我基本上只記錄重要的任務。同時，這樣能防止我接下過多工作，或承諾自己做不到的任務。現在，我總是能做到自己承諾的工作，並準時完成。

》》Q8 What information do you need before making a decision?
你在做決定之前需要哪些資訊？

Answer 8

Before I make any kind of important decision, I first consider all the surrounding facts, possible outcomes, and the desired goal. I won't hesitate to seek an outside opinion and I generally do, but I am the one who makes the ultimate decision. Once I have all the information and have weighed the risks of each possible outcome, I will make my decision.

在我做任何重要的決定之前，我首先會考慮相關的事實、可能的結果和預期的目標。我不會猶豫聽取外面的意見，而且我通常都這麼做，但我是做出最終決定的人。一旦我收集了所有資訊，並衡量了每種可能結果的風險，我就會做出決定。

》》Q9 How do you react to problems?
遇到問題，你如何反應？

Answer 9

I acknowledge their existence and respond to them in a calm manner. The problem does not get resolved until everyone calms down, accepts the situation, and then focuses on a solution.

承認問題的存在，並沉著地應對。問題不會被解決，直到所有人都冷靜下來，接受情況，然後專注在找到解決方式。

Q10 Do you consider yourself a risk taker, or do you like to play it safe?
你認為你是個喜好冒險的人，或者你喜好安穩的方式？

Answer 10

I believe that taking risks is part of life, but by mitigating the risk, I believe the best possible solution presents itself. I'm not afraid of taking risks; I just make sure that I have considered all the facts and possible outcomes my decision will have.

我認為冒險是生活的一部分，但我相信透過減少風險，最好的可能解決方式就會出現。我不怕冒險，我只是要確定我已經考慮了所有事實，以及每一個決定會造成的可能結果。

Q11 Tell me about a time you had to quickly adjust your work priorities to meet changing demands.
告訴我一個情況，是你曾必須因應變化的需求來快速調整工作先後。

Answer 11

I was in the middle of drawing up my departmental budget when I was asked to put together the costing for a big project we were tendering for. I made an outline of the information I needed immediately for the costing and assigned a portion to each of my staff. I spent the next couple of days drawing up schedules of the tasks that needed to be carried out to complete the costing, and meeting with staff members to brief them and get feedback. I was then able to re-focus on completing the budget on time. The costing was completed on time. Each staff member really contributed, and I didn't miss my budget deadline.

有一次我正在制訂部門預算時，被要求為一項我們正在投標的專案計算成本。我列了大綱，列明此成本計算我立刻需要的資料，並分配我的每個員工一人一部分。我花了接下來幾天制定任務時程表，這些任務是為了完成成本計算必須執行的，還有和員工開會簡報，以及聽取他們的回饋。然後我得以重新專注在準時完成預算制定。成本計算準時完成了。每個員工都付出努力，而我沒錯過預算的截止日。

》Q12　How do you measure talent?
你如何衡量才能？

Answer 12

Aside from defining what talent is, the organization needs to acknowledge the importance of talent, (according to the agreed organizational definitions). This requires a commitment from the very top, which must be transparent and visible to all. Then people will begin to value talent more fittingly and preciously. A similar thing happened with the "total quality" concept, when leaders woke up and realized its significance. But they first had to define it and break it down into measurable, manageable elements before they could begin to improve it. Talent is the same.

除了定義什麼是才能之外，組織需要認同才能的重要性（根據組織內達成的定義）。這需要高層給予所有員工透明、明白的承諾。然後大家就能更合適、更重視地看重才能。同樣的情況也發生在「全面品質」的觀念，領導者覺醒過來，意識到它的重要性。但在他們開始改善之前，首先他們要定義它，將其分解成可量化、可管理的要素。才能也是如此。

>> 單字片語練功坊

1. crunch　*n. [C]* 關鍵時刻；危機
2. relate to　和...有關
3. measurable　*adj.* 可量化的；可測量的
4. task　*n. [C]* 任務
5. parameter　*n. [C]* 參數
6. specify　*vt.* 具體說明
7. qualify　*vi.* 符合資格
8. distribute　*vt.* 分配；分發
9. workload　*n. [U]* 工作量
10. in the best interest of　為...的最佳利益
11. evaluate　*vt.* 評估；評價
12. empower　*vt.* 授權
13. pull one's own weight　盡自己的一份力
14. progress　*n. [C]* 進度；進步
15. keep track of　追蹤
16. spreadsheet　*n. [C]* (excel中)空白的一頁
17. overbook　*vt.* 超訂；過量

18. deliver *vt.* 傳送；遞送

19. a variety of 各種的

20. request *n. [C]* 要求

21. out of one's element 處在不相符合的環境；格格不入；
    不得其所

22. retrieve *vt.* 重新取得

23. undertaking *n. [C]* 企業；事業；工作

24. attribute *vt.* 把...歸因於

25. outcome *n. [C]* 結果

26. hesitate *vi.* 猶豫

27. ultimate *adj.* 最終的

28. acknowledge *vt.* 承認

29. resolve *vt.* 解決

30. resolution *n. [C]* 解決方法

31. play it safe 小心至上，不冒險

32. mitigate *vt.* 緩和；減輕

33. draw up 起草，制定

34. costing *n. [U]* 成本計算

35. tender for 投標

36. portion *n. [C]* 部分

37. carry out 執行；實施

38. transparent *adj.* 透明的

39. visible *adj.* 可見的

40. significance *n. [U]* 重要性

Chapter 3

📁 秘書 Secretary track 044

>> **Q1** **What sort of word documents have you been responsible for typing?**
你曾負責打字輸入哪些類型的文字檔案？

Answer 1

I performed tasks such as creating and editing tables, columns, forms and charts as well as sorting table data and performing calculations in tables.

我執行過的任務，像是製作或編輯表格、專欄、表單和圖表，還有分類表格資料，以及執行計算表格。

>> 單字片語練功坊

1. document *n. [C]* 文件
2. edit *vt.* 編輯
3. table *n. [C]* 表格
4. column *n. [C]* 專欄
5. chart *n. [C]* 圖表
6. as well as 和...
7. sort *vt.* 分類
8. calculation *n. [C]* 計算
9. format *vt.* 設計製作
10. form *n. [C]* 表單

平面設計師 **Graphic Designer** track 045

>> **Q1 Why do you want to work here?**
你為什麼想在這裡工作？

Answer 1

I would like to be a part of a company that is technologically driven and always looking towards the future. I would like to gain experience in an innovative business that has stayed ahead of the competition by foreseeing changes in the modern market.

我想在一個由科技帶動發展、並且總是展望未來的公司工作。我希望能夠獲得經驗，在一個創新的、預見現代市場變化而在競爭中領先的企業裡。

>> **Q2 Do you prefer working in a team or alone?**
你更喜歡與團隊合作還是獨立工作？

Answer 2

In my experience, joint efforts produce better results than an equal number of mutually exclusive staff. However, I have worked alone and in a team, and I enjoy both challenges. My preference is governed by which method provides the best solution to the task in hand.

在我的工作經驗中，共同的努力比同樣人數的員工獨自工作產生更好的結果。但我既獨立工作也在團隊中工作過，兩種挑戰我都很喜歡。我的偏好取決於，哪種方法對於手邊的任務提供最好的解決方式。

≫ Q3 How would you deal with criticism?
你怎麼處理批評？

Answer 3

I find constructive criticism a way of objectively analyzing my work. I try to look for the positive inside any criticism.

我認為建設性的批評是對我工作的客觀分析。我會試著在各種批評中尋找積極的一面。

≫ Q4 What are your professional strengths?
你的專業優勢是什麼？

Answer 4

As a fine-art professional, I see myself as having strong communication skills and the ability to communicate difficult design concepts in simple artistic terms. My training techniques in my previous job reduced the studying time for new graphic design software by 60%.

身為一個藝術專業人員，我認為我自己有很強的溝通能力，能用簡單地藝術術語來傳達困難的設計理念。我在先前工作中的培訓技巧使得學習新的平面設計軟體時間減少了60%。

▶▶ Q5　What is your greatest weakness?
你最大的缺點是什麼？

Answer 5

My weakness used to be that I accepted too much work in an effort to please everybody. I soon discovered that I was losing my focus and not performing as well as I should. I started to schedule my projects on a timetable base, and I did not accept more work than I could complete on time.

我以前有個缺點，就是我努力為了取悅每個人，而接下過多的工作。很快我就發現這樣讓我失去了專注力，也不能正常發揮表現。我開始用時間表規劃專案時程，並且婉拒我不能準時完成的工作。

▶▶ Q6　List your skills that would benefit this company.
列舉一下你能為這家公司帶來利益的技能。

Answer 6

I pride myself in my ability to manage, focus and motivate staff. In my previous job, I replaced a lead designer who failed to manage a difficult art project. I set the staff goals, and gave them a new focus, and finished the project on time.

我對自己能夠管理員工、讓員工集中精力、和激勵員工的能力而感到自豪。在先前的工作中，我頂替一位帶頭設計師，他無法成功管理一項困難的藝術專案。我為員工設定目標，並給他們新的工作重心，最終按時完成了任務。

Chapter 3

≫ 單字片語練功坊

1. innovation   *n. [U]* 創新
2. joint   *adj.* 共同的；聯合的
3. mutually   *adv.* 互相；彼此
4. exclusive   *adj.* 排外的；除外的
5. constructive   *adj.* 建設性的
6. criticism   *n. [U]* 批評
7. objectively   *adv.* 客觀地
8. concept   *n. [C]* 概念
9. technique   *n. [C]* 技術
10. graphic   *adj.* 繪圖的

NOTES

date: /   /

空服員 **Flight Attendant** track 046

Q1 **How do you think all you learned in school helped you prepare for a career as a flight attendant?**
你認為你在學校所學的如何幫助你準備作為空服員的職涯？

Answer 1-1

I think what I learned in school has a lot of bearing on the job. My major is related to the hospitality industry, so I learned a lot about providing people with service. You can see that I also had a minor in English. I know how important that is in this occupation.

我認為我在學校學的，很多跟此工作有關係。我的主修和服務產業有關，所以我學到很多關於提供服務的事情。您可以看到我也有副修英語。我知道那對這個職業有多麼重要。

Answer 1-2

I studied in the English department at university. Although most of the subjects were literature-related, I actually obtained excellent English ability. I know that is very important for a flight attendant.

我在大學的英文系讀書。雖然大多數的科目是和文學相關，我確實獲得了非常強的英文能力。我知道這對於成為一名空服員非常的重要。

≫ Q2 You will have to spend plenty of time in hotels waiting for your shift. Is that going to be a problem?

你將會花很多時間在飯店裡等待你的班別。這會是問題嗎？

Answer 2-1

I understand that it's not all glamour up in the air, but I am sure the rewards of getting to see different places and people will outweigh all of the negatives.

我知道這工作並不是十全十美，但我確定有機會看看不同地方和人群的報酬，將遠遠超過所有的負面因素。

Answer 2-2

No, not at all. Waiting is never a problem for me. When I was a student, I had to take the MRT to school, which usually took more than half an hour. I read some books or magazines and listened to English radio shows on the train. Time really flies when you're into something interesting.

不，一點也不會。等待對我來說從來不是問題。當我是學生時，我必須搭捷運上課，通常得花費超過半個小時。我在車廂裡讀些書或雜誌，聽英文廣播節目。當你被有趣的事物吸引時，時間真的過得很快。

≫ Q3 What would you do if a passenger complained about your service?
如果有乘客抱怨你的服務，你會怎麼做？

Answer 3-1

I would do my best to get no more complaints in the first place. I'll try to pay careful attention to the passengers and put myself in their shoes. Sometimes, people feel a little uncomfortable flying and just want a bit of personal attention. I think I would be good at doing that.

首先，我會盡我所能不要讓任何抱怨再發生。我會試著更小心地注意乘客，並為他們著想。有時候人們對飛行有點不適應，想要一點點個人的關注。我想我很擅於這麼做。

Answer 3-2

I would try to understand the passengers' needs, and ask if I could do anything more to fulfill their needs. I would also let all the other attendants on the plane know about the situation, so that the passenger would get enough attention and feel comfortable thereafter.

我會試著了解乘客的需求，並詢問是否還能做任何事來滿足他們的需求。我也會讓飛機上其他的空服員知道這個情況，讓乘客可以得到足夠的關注，之後可以感到舒適。

❯❯ Q4 Some people think that working on a plane is very dangerous. Why did you choose this job?

有人認為在飛機上工作很危險。為什麼你要選擇這份工作？

Answer 4-1

I don't think that working on a plane is dangerous. Actually, it's just as safe as any other job. We now have very advanced technology, and all the airlines are very serious about aviation safety. I don't feel that I need to be worried.

我不認為在飛機上工作是危險的，事實上，這份工作就像其他工作一樣安全。我們現在有非常先進的科技，而且所有的航空公司都非常重視飛行安全。我不覺得我需要擔心。

Answer 4-2

Every job has its risks. Working in an office might seem a lot safer than on a plane, but it's less challenging and kind of boring for me. Besides, with the latest advanced technology, I don't really think that I have to worry, and neither does any passenger.

每份工作都有其風險。在辦公室工作也許似乎比在飛機上工作安全，但比較沒有挑戰性，對我而言有點無聊。此外，隨著最新的先進科技，我並不認為我有什麼好擔心的，任何乘客根本都不需要擔心。

≫ Q5 What do you think it takes to become a good flight attendant?
你認為成為優秀的空服員需要什麼特質？

Answer 5-1

It's important that a flight attendant be willing to help. A flight attendant can face a lot of people asking for various things during the flight. I like to deal with those needs, because I always feel happy and fulfilled when I see their needs are satisfied.

空服員有樂意助人的心很重要。空服員在飛行過程中可能面對很多人要求各種事物。我喜歡處理他們的需求，因為當我看到他們的需求被滿足時，我總是感到非常開心和成就感。

Answer 5-2

I think a flight attendant should be able to stay calm at all times because there are always unexpected things during each flight. When a flight attendant looks relaxed and calm, all the passengers will feel a sense of security too.

我認為空服員應該能夠隨時保持鎮定，因為在每次的飛行中都會有意想不到的事情。當空服員看起來放鬆和鎮定時，所有的乘客也會感受到安全感。

>> **Q6** **We place a high value on discipline. Give an example of discipline in your life.**
我們很重視紀律。請舉一個你生活中紀律的例子。

Answer 6-1

I am always on time. I'm never late for any meetings or appointments. In order to do so, I always get prepared and ready ten minutes before the meeting or appointment starts.

我總是很準時，對於任何會議或約會，我從不遲到。為了達到這個結果，我總是在會議或約會開始前十分鐘就會準備就緒。

Answer 6-2

I believe a person's career and personal life are based on health, so I always run for thirty minutes a day. No matter how late I finish my shift, I never skip that.

我相信一個人的職涯和個人生活建立在健康，所以我每天總是跑步三十分鐘。無論我多晚結束工作，我從不省略。

>> **Q7** **What do you think of young people chasing after expensive things, like designer brands?**
你對時下年輕人崇尚昂貴的物品——像名牌的看法是什麼？

Answer 7

I think when a person works very hard and achieves his goal, he deserves to reward himself with something, be it a fancy dinner or an expensive handbag. However, obsession with something is a kind of addiction, and we should reward ourselves, not indulge ourselves.

我認為當一個人努力工作達到目標的時候，他值得犒賞自己，不管是很棒的晚餐或是昂貴的包包。但是，沉迷於某件事物就是一種上癮症，我們應該犒賞自己而不是放縱自己。

≫ 單字片語練功坊

1. have a lot of bearing on 和...很有關係
2. major *n. [C]* 主修
3. hospitality industry 服務業
4. minor *n. [C]* 副修
5. occupation *n. [C]* 職業；工作
6. obtain *vt.* 得到
7. glamor *n. [C]* 迷人的力量
8. outweigh *vt.* 比...更重要
9. in someone's shoes 在某人的立場
10. fulfill *vt.* 完成；實現
11. advanced *adj.* 先進的
12. sense of security 安全感
13. discipline *n. [U]* 紀律
14. appointment *n. [C]* 約定；約會
15. be based on 以...為基礎
16. skip *vt.* 跳過；省略
17. chase after 追求

Chapter 3

18. deserve　*vt.* 值得

19. obsession　*n. [C]* 著迷；執著

20. addiction　*n. [C]* 上癮

21. indulge　*vt.* 縱容

NOTES

date:　　　/　/

編輯 Editor 🔘 track 047

>> **Q1　What do you think makes a good editor?**
　　你認為什麼是一個好編輯？

Answer 1-1

It takes patience, carefulness, and focus to be a good editor. There are usually many things going on at the same time. Each and every thing can take some time, so an editor needs to be patient and not in a hurry for the outcome. The most important thing about books is accuracy, so an editor has to be very careful and find every possible mistake. Because there are many things happening, and each needs a lot of attention, an editor cannot lose his focus.

要當一位好的編輯需要耐心、細心和專注力。通常會有很多事同時要做。每件事都可能花費不少時間，所以編輯需要有耐心，不要急著看到成果。書籍最重要的就是正確，所以編輯必須很細心，找到每個可能的錯誤。因為有很多事要做，每件事都需要許多的關注，所以編輯絕不能失去他的專注力。

Answer 1-2

An editor has to be a good coordinator. We need to cooperate with the writer, the printer, the graphic designer, and others. We have to make sure that everyone does his job well and everything will be put together by the deadline.

編輯必須是一位好的協調者。我們需要和作者、印刷業者、繪圖人

員和其他人合作。我們必須確保每個人做好自己的工作，每件事在截止日期前都能完成。

>> Q2 Are you willing to work overtime?
你願意加班嗎？

Answer 2

I am a very responsible person. I always make a plan before I start, and I go with the plan in a systematic way. So, if I am behind schedule, I will definitely work overnight and make sure I will complete the project in time.

我是一個很有責任心的人，我總是在開始之前就定計畫，並且能夠系統性地按照計畫來做事。因此如果我進度比計畫慢，我一定會連夜趕工，保證我將按時完成計畫。

>> Q3 What would you do if your writer got behind in his production schedule?
如果作者延誤交稿，你會怎麼做？

Answer 3

First of all, I would try to avoid such cases before the deadline. I would make a plan for the writer to submit his works in several phases, and get in touch with him regularly to make sure he had done his job in each phase.

首先，我會在截稿日前就試著避免這種情況發生。我會替作者擬好計畫分段交稿，然後與他時常保持聯繫，確保他每個階段都完成自己的工作。

>> **Q4 Can you work on several books at the same time?**
你能夠同時處理好幾本書嗎？

Answer 4-1

Of course! I know very well that it's impossible for an editor to have only one book at one time. I'm very used to multi-tasking. Actually, I'm very good at it. In my previous job, I handled ten books at a time, and published six of them within one month.

當然，我知道一位編輯一次只處理一本書是不可能的。我非常習慣同時做很多事。實際上，我非常擅長於此。我之前的工作中，我曾一次處理十本書，而且在一個月內出版了其中的六本。

Answer 4-2

Definitely I can. At my last company, I was responsible for a monthly magazine. But at the same time, I always handled two or three books each month. I also oversaw the quality of the printer and helped come up with marketing ideas.

當然可以。在我上一個公司，我負責一本月刊。但同時我每個月總還會處理二到三本書籍。此外，我還監督印刷廠的品質以及協助發想行銷創意。

≫ Q5 How do you sell your idea to your editor-in-chief?
你如何說服總編輯接受你的想法？

Answer 5

Before I present a proposal, I will do some research on the market and the readers. I'm very sensitive to the latest developments and directions in society. Besides, I'm good at finding the right writer. I will use sufficient information and excellent analysis to submit a convincing proposal.

在我提出企劃案之前，我會進行市場調查和讀者研究。我對於社會的發展和方向非常敏銳。此外我也擅長找到對的作者。我會利用充足的資料和優質的分析來呈現具有說服力的企劃案。

≫ Q6 Can you work to a deadline?
你可以在有截稿日期下工作嗎？

Answer 6-1

Deadlines are essential to the publishing industry. If a book is not published as scheduled, it is very likely that the book will lose part of it readers. I never mind working overtime, because I know the importance of meeting the deadline.

截稿日期對出版業是必要的。如果一本書沒有照原訂時程出版，很可能這本書就會失去部分的讀者。我從不介意加班，因為我知道達成截稿目標的重要性。

Answer 6-2

Not only can I work to a deadline, I also consider the

deadline part of my work ethic. When we make a plan and decide every phase of a project, all we have to do is achieve the goal. There are definitely some unexpected situations along the way, but the goal, publishing a book on time, is never changed.

我不只能夠在截稿日期下工作，我還認為截稿日期是工作倫理的一部分。當我們擬好計畫並制定一項專案的每個階段，我們要做的就是達到目標。一路上當然會有些意想不到的情況發生，但是目標——準時出版——是絕不會改變的。

›› Q7　Do you read regularly? How often do you read?
你經常閱讀嗎？你閱讀的頻率是多常？

Answer 7-1

I like to read. That's why I want to be an editor. I like to read all kinds of books, but my favorite is fiction. I usually read a novel a month. I also subscribe to a quarterly literature magazine.

我喜歡閱讀，那就是為什麼我要當一名編輯。我喜歡閱讀各類書籍，但我最喜歡的是小說，我每個月通常讀一本小說。此外，我還訂閱了一份文學季刊。

Answer 7-2

I have the habit of reading before I sleep. Although work keeps me busy, twenty or thirty minutes every day before sleep allows me to read a book or a magazine. I don't prefer any particular kind of books, because everything I read can become part of my ideas for proposing a new book at work.

我有睡前閱讀的習慣。雖然工作讓我忙碌，每天睡前二十或三十分鐘讓我可以讀一本書或雜誌。我並不特別偏好任何一種書籍，因為我讀的任何內容都可以成為我提案新書的想法之一。

》單字片語練功坊

1. patience　*n. [U]* 耐心
2. coordinator　*n. [C]* 協調者
3. overtime　*adv.* 加班；超時
4. capability　*n. [U]* 能力
5. risky　*adj.* 有風險的
6. systematic　*adj.* 有系統的
7. behind schedule　落後
8. overnight　*adv.* 通宵；整夜
9. in time　及時
10. get in touch with　聯繫
11. phase　*n. [C]* 階段
12. oversee　*vt.* 監督；管理
13. come up with　想出
14. proposal　*n. [C]* 提案；企劃案
15. sensitive　*adj.* 敏感的；敏銳的
16. sufficient　*adj.* 足夠的
17. analysis　*n. [C]* 分析
18. ethic　*n. [C]* 倫理道德
19. subscribe to　訂閱
20. have the habit of　有...的習慣

教師 Teacher track 048

》Q1　Why did you decide to become a teacher?
你為什麼決定當老師？

Answer 1-1

The assistant principal of my high school was a real inspiration to me. Her sense of justice made me aspire to bring these things to my own classroom.
是我高中的副校長激勵了我。她的正義感使得我也想將公正等價值觀帶入我自己的課堂。

Answer 1-2

While I was student teaching, I had the opportunity to take a student aside to help him with a particularly difficult math concept that he was having trouble understanding. When I was able to show him a different way to approach the problem, and he "got it," I knew that I had chosen the right field.

有一次我教學時，有機會將一名學生帶到一旁，教他一個他不懂的困難數學概念。當我教他不同的方法來解決問題時，他懂了，那時我知道我選擇了正確的領域。

253

>> **Q2** **What type of classroom management structure would you implement if you were hired?**
如果你受聘了，你將採用何種課堂管理模式？

Answer 2

In my first grade classroom, I implemented a system where the students were each given a clip on a chart. For each infraction, the students would move their clip along a progression of colors. The disciplines ranged from a warning, losing half a recess, losing a whole recess, to a call home or to the principal's office. I made very few phone calls.

在一年級課堂，我使用這樣的管理系統，每個學生給一個迴紋針在圖表上。每違規一次，迴紋針就會在不同色彩組成的色條上移動。懲罰有警告、減少一半的休息時間、減少所有的休息時間、給家長打電話或去校長辦公室。其實我給家長打電話的次數非常少。

>> **Q3** **How have you used, or how will you use, technology in the classroom?**
關於教室中的科技產品，你曾如何使用，或將如何運用？

Answer 3

I was lucky to have one of the first "Smart Boards" in my classroom. The children were immediately engaged and eager to explore the possibilities being offered. We learned together just what an amazing teaching tool it could be.

很幸運，我曾在教室中使用過第一批「智慧白板」。孩子們很快就

被吸引投入,很想探尋它提供的潛在功能。我們一起學到了這是一個非常神奇的教學工具。

》》 Q4 Describe your disciplinary philosophy.
談談你的紀律哲學。

Answer 4

The purpose of discipline is to facilitate learning and foster better relationships and respect between the students. It is also intended to help students become more self-directed, self-disciplined, and accountable for their behavior. I have found that students respond poorly to forceful discipline, but well to discipline that is helpful. My philosophy is to provide clear limits and rules that are communicated to the students so that they have a clear understanding of what is expected of them. The rules are discussed and agreed upon to encourage accountability from the students.

紀律的目的是為了促進學習,培養學生間良好的關係和尊重。同時也是為了幫助學生成為一個自主自律的人,對自己的言行負責。我發現,學生對強制性紀律的反應不佳,而是協助性紀律的反應較佳。我的哲學是提供清楚的限制和規則,並和學生溝通好,這樣他們就能清楚地知道自己被期待做什麼事。規則會與學生們進行討論,並要得到他們的同意,以鼓勵學生的責任感。

>> **Q5 How do you handle a case of a child who is socially isolated?**
你如何處理被孤立的學生？

Answer 5

I feel I must play an important role in children's development of social competence and friendship skills. I will do my best to help these children develop peer friendships. My responsibilities involve not only imparting academic skills, but social skills as well.

我覺得我必須在孩子的社交能力和交友技巧發展方面，扮演重要的角色。我會盡最大努力去幫助這些孩子發展同儕友誼。我的責任不僅包括傳授學業技能，也包括社交能力。

>> **Q6 How do you work with the students' parents?**
你如何與學生家長合作？

Answer 6

I like to gain their trust, so they know I'm working in the child's best interest and will report to them as often as necessary. I will also make sure they know that I welcome parents' contributions.

我喜歡得到他們的信任，這樣他們知道我做一切都是為了孩子的利益，並將根據需要向家長進行回報。我也會確認他們知道我歡迎家長的付出。

》》單字片語練功坊

1. inspiration　*n. [C]* 靈感；鼓舞的人事物
2. infraction　*n. [C]* 違背；違規
3. recess　*n. [C]* 休息；休會
4. engaged　*adj.* 投入的
5. explore　*vt.* 探索；探究
6. facilitate　*vt.* 幫助；促進
7. accountable　*adj.* 有責任的
8. forceful　*adj.* 強而有力的
9. encourage　*vt.* 鼓勵
10. isolate　*vt.* 孤立
11. competence　*n. [U]* 能力
12. involve　*vt.* 包括；使涉入
13. contribution　*n. [C]* 貢獻
14. severe　*adj.* 嚴重的
15. complaint　*n. [C]* 抱怨
16. address　*vt.* 提出

NOTES

date:　　　/　/

Chapter 4
百大企業故事看板

統一企業

統一企業是台灣知名的大型食品公司，總部設在台南市。公司主要的業務是食品的製造、加工及銷售，同時並進入零售、物流、貿易、轉投資等領域。統一企業擁有許多國際知名品牌的部分經營權，例如：7-Eleven、星巴克、家樂福、無印良品、Mister Donut、Duskin、Cold Stone等。因為與跨國企業合作的豐富經驗，統一企業也自行創設了不少品牌，例如：統一夢時代購物中心、康是美藥妝店、速邁樂加油中心、二十一世紀風味館、統一速邁自販、博客來網路書店、統一渡假村、伊士邦健身俱樂部、統一速達等。

隨著旗下的轉投資事業日益壯大，加上為了更深入中國市場，因應國際化競爭的需求，統一企業從2002年開始，將集團區分為食品製

Starbucks著名logo，第一代的深褐色在1987年改為綠色，營造出明亮與活潑感，透過拉近一點的美人魚圖案，更能看清楚美人魚臉上的笑容。

造、流通、商流與貿易、投資等數個「次集團」獨立作戰，具有互相競合、資源共享的作用。統一企業的各種事業體系總合具有極高的市占率，使其在市場上享有龍頭的地位。如果統一企業調漲旗下事業體系的商品價格，對於台灣的物價波動具有一定的影響力。

在台灣之外，中國是統一企業投資規模最大的國家。統一企業自1990年代開始進入中國市場，目前已經轉投資多達五十多家

公司。此外，統一企業在越南、泰國、甚至整個東南亞地區也有投資，海內外轉投資的企業已多達一百多家。2007年12月17日，統一企業透過旗下的控股公司「統一企業中國控股有限公司」在香港掛牌上市。

◆ 更多資訊請見官網：

www.uni-president.com.tw

date: / /

UNIQLO

　　UNIQLO股份有限公司，音譯為「優衣庫」。為日本公司，創立人為柳井正先生，主力是休閒服裝設計、製造和零售。1999年2月該公司股票在東京證券交易所第一部上市。UNIQLO的產品目前是全球頂尖的平價服飾品牌，在中國大陸、香港、南韓、英國、法國、美國、台灣和馬來西亞都設有分店。

　　創業初期，UNIQLO在日本開設多間大型店面，外觀模仿美國倉庫的風格設計，店面內部則以電影海報和明星照片作為裝飾，以低價的服飾作為主力商品。1997年，UNIQLO參考美國品牌GAP的商業策略，開始設計並獨家銷售自家的成衣商品，目標集中在提供低價格、高品質的商品，並透過廣告對品牌進行宣傳。這個策略下的品牌形象轉換獲得成功，2001年8月份的營業額達到公司設立以來的高峰，同年並趁勢進軍英國市場。

　　然而2002年開始，UNIQLO在日本的庫存急速增加，在英國的業績也並不理想。隨之而來的2002年、2003年8月份業績大幅下滑。緊接著，UNIQLO買下「theory」、「national standard」等品牌，並開始與時尚雜誌合作，開發聯名商品。並且起用知名的藝人為廣告代言，也與非公司內部的設計師合作，終於在2004年成功讓營業額回升成長。

　　同時，UNIQLO也將事業版圖擴展到其他亞洲國家。尤其是2010年3月在台灣

UNIQLO台灣區總裁——Kousaka Takeshi，參加UNIQLO 2010年在台灣的開幕媒體記者會。

設立分公司，同年10月7日台灣分店開幕時，造成瘋狂搶購熱潮，引起不少話題。同年開幕的馬來西亞首家分店，也是東南亞地區最大的分店，開幕時亦造成極大的轟動，甚至有顧客在前一晚就開始排隊。

◆ 更多資訊請見官網：

www.uniqlo.com.tw

Chapter 4

NOTES

date:　　/　/

鴻海精密

鴻海精密工業股份有限公司，簡稱「鴻海精密」或「鴻海」，是台灣一家電子製造公司，也是鴻海科技集團的核心企業，創立人為郭台銘先生，於1974年創立。創立時主要從事模具製造，之後跨入電子機械代工領域，從製造連接器、電線電纜、電腦機殼、電源供應器等零件，到電腦組裝準系統與行動電話等。2001年鴻海精密的營業額打敗台積電，成為台灣第一大的民營企業。2005年更超越國營公司中油，成為台灣最大企業。

鴻海透過提供全球最具競爭力的「全方位成本優勢」，使電腦、通訊、3C產品成為便利生活的一部分。具備機光電垂直整合、一次購足整體解決方案的代工優勢。其五大產品策略為「速度、品質、工程服務、效率、附加價值」。

2003年富比士雜誌公布的全球四百大企業，上榜的台灣公司中，鴻海是營收排名最高的。鴻海近幾年快速發展，成為台灣民營企業的龍頭。鴻海於1977年赴大陸投資，現今已成為大陸台商的第二大出口商。隨著成本競爭的優勢，以及研發技術提高，獲利更是逐年提升。

鴻海在大陸的主要製造基地是富士康集團，主要生產電腦、網路通訊、消費性電子等關鍵零組件與系統產品。在中國大陸深圳、昆山、杭州、天津等地設有36家全資子公司。位於深圳的富士康集團是鴻海在大陸的公司，在2001年出口額達24億美元，占深圳當年出口總值的6.2%。

◆ 更多資訊請見官網：

www.foxconn.com.tw

王品集團

　　王品集團的董事長為戴勝益先生，成立王品於1990年，在台中市文心路開設第1家王品台塑牛排。自成立後，業務快速擴張，先後經營王品台塑牛排、外蒙古全羊大餐、一品肉粽、金氏世界紀錄博物館等，經營領域橫跨餐飲、樂園等各種事業。

　　2001年王品開始進入美國市場，策略布局的同時，發現事業定位模糊，因此切斷與集團不相干的事業，集中焦點深耕。聚焦餐飲業，以「多品牌經營」讓旗下的企業發揮所長。為了讓品牌經營無後顧之憂，則制訂標準化規則、輔佐經營、研究發展、行銷布局、人力資源等，讓每個品牌創造更佳業績。從第一家王品牛排開幕，到現在年營業額突破五十億元，成為台灣餐飲業第一名的企業集團。公司目前資本額4億，員工約有3,400人，陸續開創10個王品集團的旗下企業餐飲連鎖品牌。

　　王品成功的關鍵就是其人性為本的企業文化。以「一家人主義」出發，對員工無微不至的照顧與真誠關懷，一直到完整的教育訓練與終身學習，以及鼓勵創意的內在文化，員工甚至還有內部創業的機會。

　　王品集團積極布局兩岸市場，目前台灣11個品牌共227家店，2013年目標至300店；大陸5個品牌共59家店，今年將再新增1品牌、至少22家新店為目標。飲食連鎖方面全部直營，而且都是「無負債經營」。 王品擁有優質的文化與連鎖餐飲的制度，2006年營收43億新台幣營業額，勝過晶華酒店、統一星巴克、君悅酒店等國際品牌。

◆ 更多資訊請見官網：

www.wangsteak.com.tw

宏達國際電子

　　宏達國際電子股份有限公司，簡稱「宏達電」、「HTC」，是智慧型手機與平板電腦自有品牌製造商，為威盛電子轉投資的公司。宏達電是開放手機聯盟的創始成員之一，現由王雪紅女士擔任董事長。2008年6月，公司的正式英文名稱從High Tech Computer Corporation更名為HTC Corporation。

　　宏達電早期專注於代工業務，2002年開始生產全球第一台搭載微軟Smartphone 2002平台的智慧型手機，一度擁有Windows Mobile智慧型手機80%市場。2006年開始推出自創品牌的智慧型手機，在2011年發展迅速，成為全球知名手機生產商。2012年，HTC在世界手機市場以1.8%的市占率位列第10。

　　宏達電成立於西元1997年5月，並於2002年掛牌上市；2005年2月以股價232元首度超越聯發科技，登上股王寶座。於2009年宣布推出新的品牌定位Quietly Brilliant，並推出該主題第一支全球廣告。宏達電於2005年和2006年分別在歐洲和日本開設分公司。

◆ 更多資訊請見官網：
　www.htc.com/tw/

華碩電腦

　　華碩電腦股份有限公司，簡稱「華碩」，品牌為「ASUS」，成立於1990年，是全球最大的主機板製造商，並為全球第三大筆記型電腦公司，也是顯示卡、桌上電腦、通訊產品、光碟機等產品的領導廠商，目前董事長為施崇棠先生。

　　華碩在2008年將公司切割為「品牌」和「代工」兩個集團，和碩聯合科技（Pegatron）負責電腦產品相關代工事業體，永碩聯合國際（Unihan）負責機殼、寬頻等非電腦產品相關代工事業體。華碩公司主機板，筆記型電腦與顯示卡產品在國際上具有非常強的競爭力。

　　華碩持續為消費者及企業用戶提供嶄新的科技解決方案，2012年獲得全球專業媒體與評鑑機構共4,168個獎項的肯定。2011年，華碩推出市場高評價的變形平板。2012年發表結合手機、平板、小筆電跨界功能的PadFone，奠定華碩的研發創新實力。目前，華碩積極布局未來的行動雲端時代。在著重創新與品質之餘，華碩亦投注心力於社會公益、教育文化及綠色環保等方面，並在歐洲、美國、日本及台灣本地等國際環保標章上，領先取得多項肯定與認證。

◆ 更多資訊請見官網：
　www.asus.com/tw/

Chapter 4

267

台積電

　　台灣積體電路製造股份有限公司，簡稱「台積電」，英文簡寫為TSMC。成立於1987年，是全球第一家、也是全球最大的專業積體電路製造服務（晶圓代工）公司。在2011年時，該公司的晶圓代工市占率是48.8%，為全球第一。台積電在台灣證券交易所，以及紐約股票交易所皆上市。2011年的資本額約新台幣2,591.5億元，市值約2兆5689億元，是台灣股市中市值最大的公司。

　　台積電的董事長兼執行長為張忠謀先生。2011年台積電全球員工總數為32,707人。台積電的全球總部位於新竹科學園區，透過與客戶所建立的穩定夥伴關係，創造堅強而有力的成長。全球的IC供應商因信任台積電的製程技術、設計服務、製造生產力與產品品質，將其產品交由台積電生產。客戶服務與業務代表的據點包括台灣新竹、台中、台南、日本橫濱、印度邦加羅爾、韓國首爾、荷蘭阿姆斯特丹、美國聖荷西及橙郡、德州奧斯汀，以及麻州波士頓等地。

　　台積電透過遍及全球的營運據點，服務全世界的半導體市場。台積電立基台灣，目前擁有三座最先進的十二吋晶圓廠、四座八吋晶圓廠、以及一座六吋晶圓廠。公司總部、晶圓二廠、三廠、五廠、八廠和晶圓十二廠等各廠，皆位於新竹科學園區，而晶圓六廠以及十四廠則位於台南科學園區，另一座十二吋廠位於台中科學園區的晶圓十五廠。此外，台積電亦有轉投資子公司美國華盛頓州的WaferTech公司、在中國上海的台積電有限公司，以及新加坡與NXP合資的SSMC公司充沛的產能支援。

◆ 更多資訊請見官網：

www.tsmc.com/chinese/default.htm

 中華電信

　　中華電信股份有限公司，簡稱中華電信、中華電，是台灣最大的電信服務業者，業務範圍涵蓋固網通訊、數據通訊及行動通訊等。

　　1996年依據電信三法，交通部電信總局的電信事業營運部門正式成為國營公司，名為中華電信股份有限公司，隸屬於交通部。中華電信成立時，資本額為新台幣964.77億元，經營第一類及第二類電信業務，為民營化奠立基礎。從此以後，電信總局專責電信行政監督，中華電信專責電信事業之經營。

　　2000年10月，中華電信於台灣證券交易所上市。2003年7月，中華電信於紐約證券交易所上市。2005年8月12日，中華電信的政府持股降至50％以下，正式成為民營公司。目前中華電信是台灣規模最大的電信公司，提供全方位的電信服務。

　　2007年5月1日，中華電信成立「企業客戶分公司」，中華電信台灣中區電信分公司併入台灣南區電信分公司。2009年，中華電信裁撤「數位內容處」，MOD業務由總公司移轉至台灣北區電信分公司負責。

◆ 更多資訊請見官網：
www.cht.com.tw

天下雜誌

　　天下雜誌是台灣第一份以財經為主要導向的綜合性雜誌。創立於1981年6月1日，正逢美國和中華民國斷交之際。當時擔任華爾街日報駐台記者的殷允芃女士，認為台灣必須透過經濟發展以突破困境，因此與高希均先生、王力行女士共同創辦天下雜誌，專門報導財經相關的新聞。至今其報導範圍已擴及一般民生、歷史與教育領域，旗下並且還有三份期刊。

　　天下雜誌主要報導台灣經濟金融、企業經營、產業趨勢等新聞。報導內容以財經為主軸，以社會環境、人文教育及環境保護為輔。另外，定期推出台灣「一千大企業排名」、「標竿企業排名」、「企業社會公民CSR」、「兩岸三地調查」、「金牌服務大賞」等調查，享有極高的公信力。

　　天下雜誌創刊時採月刊形式發行，自第254期改為半月刊，第338期起再改為雙週刊迄今，每隔週三出刊。此外，天下雜誌每年出版三冊教育專刊，並且跨足電視傳播媒介，於2013年與公視基金會談話性節目「有話好說」首次合作。

◆ 更多資訊請見官網：

www.cw.com.tw

長榮航空

　　長榮航空是台灣第二大的民用航空業者，為長榮集團成員，總部位於桃園南崁，同時提供客運與貨運服務，航點遍布亞洲、澳洲、歐洲和北美洲。子公司立榮航空則負責國內和區域性航線。長榮航空於2013年加入星空聯盟，成為第二間加入國際航空聯盟的台灣籍航空業者。

　　1988年9月，長榮海運在慶祝成立20周年之時，董事長張榮發先生宣布，將建立台灣第一間私人的國際航空公司。在獲得官方批准後，長榮航空公司於1989年3月正式成立，砸下36億美元向波音公司和麥道公司購買共26架飛機，1991年正式投入營運。一開始以台北為出發地，目的地包含曼谷、雅加達、新加坡和吉隆坡。同年底，長榮航空的網絡已擴大到其他東亞城市，以及歐洲航線的維也納。

　　長榮航空於2007年宣布台北直飛紐約紐瓦克機場的航班。2008年7月每週兩岸包機的服務啟動後，長榮也依據兩岸三通的協議，增加直飛大陸地區的航班。在2007年時，長榮航空的載客量達到620萬。另外，長榮航空在2012年與星空聯盟簽署加盟協議書，於2013年6月18日正式加入。

此外，喜歡Hello Kitty的朋友一定不會忘記長榮航空的Kitty 彩繪機，從機身到內裝，通通都有可愛的Kitty身影，長榮航空與日本三麗鷗合作推出Kitty彩繪機，有魔法機、蘋果機、環球機、歡樂機、雲彩機，也推出相關行程和紀念品，在機場航廈裡還有規劃Kitty專區，成功擄獲許多大朋友和小朋友的目光。在2013年請來國際知名巨星金城武拍攝品牌廣告 "I See You"，再次成功引起話題與討論。

◆ 更多資訊請見官網：

www.evaair.com

NOTES

date:　　　/　/

📁 誠品書店

　　誠品書店為台灣的大型連鎖書店之一，創辦人為吳清友先生，創立於1989年。第一家店座落於台北市的敦化南路，早期以販售藝術、人文方面的書籍為主。隨後陸續開設多家分店，並且成立誠品商場，而跨足百貨零售業。

　　誠品書店的名稱eslite是由法文而來，為「菁英」之意。而中文取名「誠品」，代表誠品對於美好社會的追求與實踐。誠品書店本身對於所謂「菁英」的定義是：「努力活出自己生命中精彩的每一個人」。

　　誠品集團在2011年的營業收入當中，7成的收入是來自商場業務，書店的部分則佔3成，造訪書店的人次高達1億2千萬人。

　　誠品書局在台灣各地設有分店，當中台北市的敦南店為24小時營業，也是許多外國遊客來台的熱門景點之一。「誠品香港銅鑼灣店」於2012年在香港銅鑼灣希慎廣場開業，面積達3.6萬平方呎。其中85%賣書，其餘則為餐廳、茶室及設計品的展售空間。

　　誠品書局計畫在3到5年之內於香港再開立3到5間分店，首選地點為中環或尖沙嘴等人流較多的地區。而誠品集團的下一步發展則是拓展中國市場，蘇州店預計在2014年開幕。

◆ 更多資訊請見官網：

www.eslite.com

誠品總經理——吳旻潔小姐，為誠品創辦人吳清友先生的女兒。

好書搶先報

麥禾陽光 Sun&Wh

2013.7 上市！

財商智庫03

關鍵報告：誰是老闆心中的最愛？
Whom does your boss admire most?
是你？是他？勇敢舉手用力大喊 "It's ME!"

優秀的人力是企業最大的資產；成功的企業與優秀的員工之間的關係，就像是魚幫水、水幫魚的道理，兩者相互依賴，缺一不可。職場成功的基礎，絕對與成為一名優秀、傑出的員工脫不了關係，腳踏實地、一步一腳印，必能往成功之路邁進。

美國總統杜魯門上任後，在自己的辦公桌上擺了個牌子，上面寫著 "Bucket stop here!"，意思就是「讓自己負起責任來，不要把問題丟給別人」。這句話展現一種積極的心態，也點出了如何正確面對問題的方法和技巧。想要提升職場競爭力、想要變身優秀人力、想要變成老闆心中的最愛的你千萬不能錯過！

JOB

忘記怨恨不是承受創痛，
而是選擇為自己療傷…

學會感恩不是徒增負擔，
而是讓自己更加完美。

財商智庫04

Yes! 愈感謝，愈快樂！

The more GRATEFUL you are, the more JOYFUL you will be!

善緣、貴人、正面能量全都來自於感謝的力量，一個你不得不相信的事實。

如果你最近有點「失溫」……
如果你最近的生活有點空虛……
如果你最近老覺得都沒有貴人幫助……
——你需要一杯咖啡和一本有「溫度」的書。

忙碌的生活讓大家的心也跟著一直往前走，很難有機會能稍作休息，於是乎我們很容易忽略了我們最親的家人、朋友，忙碌的你有多久沒有跟你身邊的人好好說聲：「謝謝你」了呢？

用一顆更寬厚且感恩的心，面對煩瑣生活中的挫敗和挑戰；卸下怨恨，學會感恩，做一個真正快樂的人。愛——是我們與生俱來的本能，而感謝更是我們潛在的能力，一個小小的改變與調整，轉個角度，將會看到一個全然不同的世界！

職場 ♥ 英文 001

我是英語面試人氣王！
A step-by-step GUIDE to a WINNING INTERVIEW.
—— 掌握英語面試技巧，立馬擁抱理想工作！

作　　者 / 徐維克
總 編 輯 / Estelle Chen
特約編輯 / 林怡璇
外籍專審 / Mark Venekamp
封面設計 / 陳小KING
內頁構成 / 麥禾陽光文化出版社
圖片出處 / www.dreamstime.com
印　　製 / 世和印製企業有限公司
出　　版 / 麥禾陽光文化出版社
總 經 銷 / 易可數位行銷股份有限公司
地　　址 / 231 新北市新店區寶橋路 235 巷 6 弄 3 號 5 樓
電　　話 / (02) 8911-0825
傳　　真 / (02) 8911-0801
初　　版 / 2013 年 8 月
定　　價 / 新台幣 349 元

國家圖書館出版品預行編目 (CIP) 資料

我是英語面試人氣王 / 徐維克著.
　初版. -- 新北市：麥禾陽光文化, 2013.08
　面； 　公分
　ISBN 978-986-89735-0-3 (平裝附光碟片)

　1. 英語　2. 會話　3. 面試

805.188　　　　　　　　　　　　102013274

麥禾陽光 *Sun&Wheat*

一個溫暖、高質感、充滿趣味的閱讀環境，
帶給讀者一個全然不同的學習感受。

麥禾陽光 *Sun&Wheat*

一個溫暖、高質感、充滿趣味的閱讀環境，
帶給讀者一個全然不同的學習感受。

麥禾陽光 *Sun&Wheat* ━━━━━━━━━━━━━━━●

一個溫暖、高質感、充滿趣味的閱讀環境,
帶給讀者一個全然不同的學習感受。

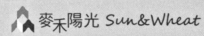

麥禾陽光 Sun&Wheat

一個溫暖、高質感、充滿趣味的閱讀環境，
帶給讀者一個全然不同的學習感受。

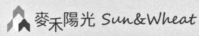

麥禾陽光 Sun&Wheat

一個溫暖、高質感、充滿趣味的閱讀環境，
帶給讀者一個全然不同的學習感受。

麥禾陽光 Sun&Wheat

一個溫暖、高質感、充滿趣味的閱讀環境,
帶給讀者一個全然不同的學習感受。